‖‖‖ ‖‖‖‖‖‖‖‖‖‖‖‖‖‖‖‖‖‖‖‖‖‖‖‖‖

✍ **W9-AMC-237**

"I'm not some mindless slave to sex."

Skye continued, "There has to be more to it."

"It wasn't just sex," Nick said harshly. "Do you really see it like that?"

"It wasn't much more."

Nick Hunter watched her walk away and ground his teeth in sheer frustration as he asked himself why the hell he couldn't just let Skye Belmont go.

The thing was, he mused savagely, there was no way he could transform himself into the kind of husband she wanted.

So why, he asked himself, did he feel as if he'd let her down?

LINDSAY ARMSTRONG was born in South Africa, but now lives in Australia with her New Zealand-born husband and their five children. They have lived in nearly every state of Australia and tried their hand at some unusual, for them, occupations, such as farming and horse training—all grist to the mill for a writer! Lindsay started writing romances when their youngest child began school and she was left feeling at a loose end. She is still doing it and loving it.

THE BRIDEGROOM'S DILEMMA

LINDSAY ARMSTRONG

THE MARRIAGE QUEST

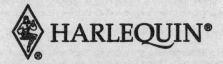

HARLEQUIN®

TORONTO • NEW YORK • LONDON
AMSTERDAM • PARIS • SYDNEY • HAMBURG
STOCKHOLM • ATHENS • TOKYO • MILAN • MADRID
PRAGUE • WARSAW • BUDAPEST • AUCKLAND

If you purchased this book without a cover you should be aware that this book is stolen property. It was reported as "unsold and destroyed" to the publisher, and neither the author nor the publisher has received any payment for this "stripped book."

ISBN 0-373-80625-6

THE BRIDEGROOM'S DILEMMA

First North American Publication 2003.

Copyright © 2000 by Lindsay Armstrong.

All rights reserved. Except for use in any review, the reproduction or utilization of this work in whole or in part in any form by any electronic, mechanical or other means, now known or hereafter invented, including xerography, photocopying and recording, or in any information storage or retrieval system, is forbidden without the written permission of the publisher, Harlequin Enterprises Limited, 225 Duncan Mill Road, Don Mills, Ontario, Canada M3B 3K9.

All characters in this book have no existence outside the imagination of the author and have no relation whatsoever to anyone bearing the same name or names. They are not even distantly inspired by any individual known or unknown to the author, and all incidents are pure invention.

This edition published by arrangement with Harlequin Books S.A.

® and TM are trademarks of the publisher. Trademarks indicated with ® are registered in the United States Patent and Trademark Office, the Canadian Trade Marks Office and in other countries.

www.eHarlequin.com

Printed in U.S.A.

CHAPTER ONE

'LOOK at this! I don't believe it.' The middle-aged man lowered his newspaper and stared at his companion. 'Skye Belmont and Nick Hunter have broken off their engagement only three weeks before the wedding!'

'Doesn't surprise me,' the second man sitting at the pavement café said thoughtfully as he stirred his cappuccino. 'Two very high-profile people, big egos, no doubt.' He shrugged.

'One very beautiful, high-profile person and *she* doesn't act as if she has a big ego,' the first man said with a sigh. 'You know, Skye Belmont is the one girl I'd leave *everything* for. Those wonderful, laughing blue eyes, gorgeous figure, skin like satin, curly hair—I reckon she's a natural blonde—and her legs are something to die for.'

His friend looked amused. 'Wouldn't we all? And they did seem like the perfect couple, but you never can tell.'

'If he's hurt her…' the first man said pugnaciously.

'Could be the other way around.'

'Not Skye. She's such a honey!'

'Oh, well, we'll probably never know…'

'Skye, you can't sit there all day, darling.'

Skye Belmont stirred and looked around her bedroom. She flinched visibly as her gaze fell on her beautiful wedding dress hanging up outside the wardrobe door then she glanced up at her mother. 'If you must know, Mum, I wish there was a handy hole in the ground for me to hide in!'

Her mother sat down on the end of the bed and said gently, 'You were the one who broke it off, Skye. For a lot of very good reasons, you told me. And all this interest and publicity will die down. Don't forget, it was inevitable. Are you not the most sought-after cook-show host in town? And is Nick not—'

'The most eligible bachelor in town,' Skye finished for her mother wearily. She laid her head back and two tears trickled down her cheeks. 'Don't I know it.'

'Skye, are you regretting it now?' her mother asked anxiously.

'No.' Skye licked the salty moisture from her lip. 'But just between you and me, Mum, even though I know I can't live with him and—all the rest, I guess I might always miss him.'

Iris Belmont looked concerned. 'There's an old saying: The devil you know...' She raised a delicate eyebrow at her daughter as she left the saying unfinished.

Skye smiled faintly. 'If there's someone who can cope with the devil in Nick, it's not me.'

'You're on the front page this morning, Mr Hunter,' Florence Daley said as she slapped a sheaf of newspapers in front of her boss.

Nick Hunter removed his feet from his desk, his hands from behind his head and sat up with a sigh.

He was six feet two with straight, short, almost black hair and eyes. Beneath the dark grey shirt he wore with a jade-green tie and charcoal trousers, his shoulders were broad and there was an air of suppressed energy about him despite the fact that he'd been lounging with his feet up, so immobile and deep in thought.

The rest of him was lean, rangy and unobtrusively powerful, but the most arresting thing was his face. You never stopped to wonder whether he was handsome, Florence thought, because there was so much vitality, humour yet strength in it. When he laughed, it was almost impossible not to laugh with him. When he raised an eyebrow with utter arrogance at you, you immediately felt demolished. No wonder she hadn't been able to cope, the poor kid...

'I suppose the whole world is wondering what kind of a bastard I am to have ditched Skye?' he drawled, breaking in on her reflections.

'Yes,' his secretary said severely.

'Not you too, Flo!' He eyed Florence injuredly. She was in her early sixties, she always displayed a very prim and proper demeanour and, as his father's secretary originally, she had known him since he was sixteen.

'Me too, I'm afraid,' Florence agreed. 'I *love* Skye and I thought you did as well.'

'Loving Skye and marrying Skye,' Nick Hunter said meditatively, 'are two different things. By the way, it was she who gave me my marching orders.'

'I wonder why?' Florence said with unusual irony. And proceeded to tell him. 'You're never here, for one thing! It would be like being married to a long-distance telephone. And you're always doing difficult, dangerous things you don't *have* to do—she'd never know when the father of her children would turn up as a statistic! Plus...' Florence paused then went on with unusual vehemence, 'Too many women are attracted to you and make fools of themselves over you.'

Nick had listened to this attentively but his dark eyebrows shot up at the last two observations. He said, with a grin, 'Flo, I do think you're exaggerating there—'

But Florence was in the grip of high emotion and would not be denied. 'Nor does it become you to joke about it, Nicholas Hunter,' she snapped. 'The trouble with you is you've always had everything handed to you on a platter and you're too used to dominating the life out of everyone around you.'

'Is that what you think? That I tried to dominate Skye?'

'Wouldn't put it past you.'

They gazed at each other until Florence reddened suddenly and looked away. 'Sorry,' she said stiffly, 'it's not my place—'

'No.' Nick waved a hand. 'You're perfectly entitled to speak your mind. If nothing else it's brought one thing home to me. As I'm going to feature as the villain of the piece, it might be a good idea to leave town for a while.'

'You're still...you're being flippant,' Florence pointed out frustratedly. 'Didn't she mean anything to you?'

It was Nick's turn to look away and for a moment there was something entirely serious, even dark about him. But he broke the moment with a faint smile, and said almost gently, 'Flo, I will always love Skye in a way. But, for reasons that matter only to the two of us, we would not suit. Surely it's better to have found this out before the wedding?'

'You need to get away for a while, darling,' Iris Belmont said to her daughter over dinner that same evening. 'Doesn't this series of the show close shortly for a recess? That usually gives you three months before you start taping the next series, or something like that.'

'Yes. But there's still work to be done on the next series, my new book...' Skye inspected her meal then pushed her plate away. 'Sorry, I'm not hungry, Mum.'

'You could work on your new book anywhere,' Iris pointed out. 'You might make even pick up some new ideas for it.'

'I guess so. Look—' Skye stood up '—I'll think about it,' she promised. 'In the meantime I'm going to have an early night. Please don't worry about me. I'm...I'll be fine!'

Famous last words, she thought as she lay on her bed in the house she'd grown up in and had retreated to after breaking her engagement. She had her own flat not that far away but, apart from being alone, which her mother had insisted she shouldn't be, being prey to the media hadn't recommended itself to her.

It was a blue room, her bedroom in her mother's house. Blue to match her eyes, frilly and appropriate for a little girl but not much comfort for a woman who had loved and lost Nick Hunter.

She let her mind drift back to how they'd met over a year ago. Cooking had always been her passion, a passion passed onto her by her mother. After her father's death when she was twenty, she and her mother had invested their inheritance into a small, chic restaurant that had taken off overnight.

And one of their regular clients, a television producer, had offered Skye a guest spot on a cooking program. Before she'd had time to pinch herself, she often thought, she had her own show that worked on a tried, not particularly original formula but it *had* worked amazingly well. She went into the home of a celebrity, took over the kitchen and cooked their favourite dishes for them.

What had puzzled her at first was the metamorphosis that came over her when she was in front of the cameras. She'd always been a reserved person, her teens had been plagued by shyness and she'd had a very sheltered childhood. Yet on the small screen she came across as bubbly, worldly, humorous and able to make people laugh—and before long, at twenty-two, she'd been unable to go to the supermarket without being recognized.

She'd discussed this paradox with her producer and he'd pointed out that by all accounts Rowan Atkinson was a shy, reserved person. He'd also told her that it was her passion for her subject that gave her her on-air confidence. And assured her that the way she dealt with her celebrities flowed on from it.

Off-screen confidence in some areas had also gradually flowed from it, she'd found, although fame and constantly being recognized had proved to be a bit of a problem. On the other hand, fame and a relative amount of fortune had seen her able to hire help for the restaurant, although her mother still supervised it, and had seen her first cookbook leap off the shelves.

Then, one day, it was in Nick Hunter's kitchen that she'd found herself doing a show. Of course she'd heard of him. His father was reputed to be one of the wealthiest men in the country. His mother was a renowned psychologist. His sister designed couturier clothes and lived in Paris. He himself was second-in-command of the vast empire his father had carved mainly from minerals.

He flew his own plane around the country, had a passion for motor racing as well as speedboats and competed as an amateur. In fact anything fast and racy, including women, often appeared in the same context as Nick Hunter.

She'd been surprised, therefore, when he'd immediately divined her determination to be unimpressed by him behind the scenes. And more surprised when, by a mysterious process, he'd turned their on-air time into one of the best shows she'd ever done. Hilarious, warm and as if a certain chemistry existed between them as she showed him how to boil an egg.

She could even remember saying indignantly to her mother when they'd watched the show together, 'How did he do that? He's not the kind of man who impresses me at all.'

Her mother had looked quizzical. 'He's rather gorgeous, though. I mean physically,' she'd amended hastily, discovering herself on the receiving end of a speaking look from her daughter.

'He's also a playboy if I'm not very much mistaken,' Skye had said coolly.

'Oh, to be sure. A right breaker of hearts, I have no doubt. Lucky you're not an impressionable girl, Skye,' Iris had added, but with a little twinkle in her eye that had caused her daughter to look affronted then start to laugh reluctantly.

'OK—tall, dark and dangerously attractive,' she'd conceded ruefully. 'He still, well, puts my hackles up.'

What had further put her hackles up was to discover that the ratings for the Hunter show had been astronomical, causing her to be the blue-eyed girl of the station in more ways than one.

She'd remonstrated with herself over this state of mind. She was being ridiculous and, if anything, she should have bought the most expensive bottle of champagne she could find for Nick Hunter—only he'd got in first. With flowers and a lunch invitation.

Go! everyone had insisted. But what had made her go, she'd thought at the time, was a determination to prove to Nick that she could remain unimpressed by him.

Now, as she lay dry-eyed but miserable on her bed, she had to acknowledge that she'd probably been impressed from the first time his dark eyes had lingered on her. From the moment he'd unwound his tall, spare frame from a low armchair and run his fingers through his straight dark hair when she and the television crew had descended upon him.

And going to lunch with him that first time had definitely been a mistake, in hindsight, she also conceded.

Because he'd done nothing at all to cement her playboy image of him—the opposite if anything. He'd told her about his particular passion—for rocks, as it happened. He was a geologist, he told her, and, be they iron ore, gold, silver, tin or diamond-bearing rocks, he found them exceedingly fascinating. He'd also told her he was never happier than when he was prospecting, living in a tent somewhere.

Prepared for a sophisticated, seductive onslaught of some kind, she had relaxed unwittingly. Three hours later, she'd been unable to believe the time had passed so swiftly, or been so interesting.

And Nick Hunter had watched the slight confusion that came to her expression with a little glint of something she couldn't identify at the time in his dark eyes.

Because he *was* aware that beneath her TV persona there lurked a different Skye Belmont; he had divined it at their first encounter when her beautiful sky-blue eyes had been distinctly cool. And, although he couldn't put his finger on it, it had been enough to intrigue him. In what way could she be different underneath from all the other bright, worldly girls who littered his path? And if so—why?

Had Skye been privy to his thoughts at the time, she would have known that he also knew exactly how to reel her in... It was something she was later to throw up at him.

He'd ended the lunch on a friendly, casual note,

made no reference to their meeting again and left her with an oddly intimate handshake. She hadn't heard from him again for two months.

For the first week of those two months she'd been strangely insulated from just about everything, work included. Because she couldn't get over how much she'd enjoyed Nick Hunter's company, how ordinary it had been—yet not ordinary at all. He'd been witty, serious, he'd got her to talk about her opinions on books, films, politics, and had responded in kind. It had been like having lunch with a very good friend.

At the same time, though, there'd been this sudden awareness of him flowing through her. Not, at first, in a particularly sensual way but little things—such as how she liked that he was lean and rangy, she liked his hands and the way he smiled, his voice. It had only occurred to her after they'd parted that just once his dark eyes had rested on her in a way that was particularly adult.

It had been in the moment of confusion when she'd realized they'd spent three whole hours together. And that drifting gaze had, almost objectively, she thought later, seen through her clothes but, more, read her soul.

This discovery had caused her to shiver slightly for a reason she couldn't explain, but the more she thought about it, the more she saw it as a danger sign—and the more everything about Nick Hunter started to plague her. Then the weeks had passed and her feeling of friendship, already eroded, had hardened into something she despised herself for but couldn't help—sheer pique.

So the fact that he caught her completely unprepared two months after their lunch, and not as the result of him getting in touch with her, didn't help her much.

She tried, as she lay on her bed, to resist being transported back in time to that meeting but it was useless...

'Going my way, lady?'

The voice was the voice of her rather bitter dreams but it brought her up short in the act of stepping into a lift in a smart city hotel, on her way to a cocktail party to celebrate the release of a new wine.

She turned slowly with her heart suddenly pounding, and Nick Hunter was standing behind her, all the lean length of him clad in black: black open-necked shirt, black trousers and with his straight dark hair flopping on his forehead.

'Oh, it's you,' she said unoriginally, although she wasn't unhappy with the lack of enthusiasm in her voice.

'Mmm,' he murmured, letting his gaze drift over her in that disturbing way he had, 'and a very beautiful-looking you, Ms Belmont. But cool. Distinctly cool...'

The word seemed to dangle in the air between them as she looked down at herself in some confusion.

She wore a short, bias-cut dress with a vee neck in a floating silk georgette over a taffeta slip. The cap sleeves were unlined, the colour was a beautiful Prussian blue with a shadowy dusky pink pattern on it and she wore silver high-heeled sandals. Her long, slender legs were bare and her fair hair was in its natural curly bob to her shoulders. She wore a minimum of make-up and her lips were painted a dusky pink. All she carried was a tiny blue purse.

'Should I be any different?' she asked, having used the moment to banish the confusion and starch her soul against this man, as their gazes caught and held again.

He smiled, as if with inner amusement that she might not be adult enough to be privy to, and said, 'I thought we were friends? We certainly seemed to be the last time we met.'

Skye blinked, conscious immediately of the trap she'd fallen into, and for a moment her expression defied description.

This time Nick Hunter laughed softly. But at the same time he possessed himself of her hand. 'Look, I've been overseas. For quite a bit longer than I'd originally planned, I'm afraid. Would it be too much to hope that we're going to the same cocktail party?'

Skye opened her mouth, shut it then said, 'I'm going to the launch of this new wine. I don't know about you.'

He laughed again and ushered her into the lift. 'I am now.'

She stared at him. 'Do you mean…?'

'Precisely,' he drawled. 'I intend to come to the wine party with you.'

'But if you haven't got an invitation—and what about the one you were invited to anyway?'

'I never seem to have any trouble getting into parties whether I'm invited or not,' he commented gravely. 'And the one I was going to will be deadly dull in comparison—'

'So why…?'

'Because *you* won't be there,' he finished softly.

Skye blushed and he watched the colour surge beneath her smooth skin, which had the effect of making her feel hotter than ever.

But as she cast around in her mind for a suitable rejoinder he grimaced, kissed her knuckles lightly and said, 'Shall we be friends again?'

He was right. He was more than welcome at the cocktail party; the producers of the new wine were even old friends of his, and they lamented loudly that they hadn't known he was in the country otherwise they'd have sent him an invitation.

And Skye watched, somewhat bemused, because Nick Hunter in action at a party was a sight to behold. Everyone seemed to know him and be delighted to see him. Including some very attractive women who hung on his every word.

But, after about an hour, he came back to Skye's side and said for her ears alone, 'I've had rather a good idea. Shall we go?'

She moistened her lips. 'Where?'

He narrowed his eyes. 'I wonder why I get the impression Skye Belmont has never lived a little dangerously?'

'Believe me, I have,' she countered. 'Every time I go in front of a camera I might as well be white-water rafting down the Zambezi in crocodile-infested waters—that's how nervous I get.'

His lips quirked and his eyes glinted with amusement. 'You don't show it.'

'Perhaps not. I feel it all the same. The funny thing is, as soon as the cameras are rolling, I lose it. But—' she shrugged her slim shoulders '—I am cautious by nature. So, before I make any commitment, how dangerously are you asking me to live at the moment, Nick Hunter?' Her own eyes were a cool, amused blue.

His changed to reflect a glimmer of surprise but he was not to know that Skye had learnt a thing or two in the preceding hour. She had accurately perceived that he very quickly divested himself of women who could not hide their admiration of him.

'All I had in mind was you doing something you've done for me before—cooking me dinner,' he said. 'Which was not dangerous at all, if you remember. And I happen to have a refrigerator stuffed with food—but you know how hopeless I am in the kitchen,' he added helplessly.

Skye's lips twitched. 'Ah. But I was paid for that.'

'Then could you consider this?' He glanced around. 'Little bites of food on toothpicks always leave me the same way. Starving,' he said simply.

'You could go to a restaurant,' she pointed out.

'When I know the best cook in town? That would be sacrilege,' he said softly. 'But, I give you my word, I'll deliver you home all safe and sound.'

Skye hesitated but she couldn't help laughing at his expression, which was an entirely false mixture of pleading and mournfulness. 'OK.' She shrugged. 'I don't know why I don't always go out armed with an apron!'

'This…' he paused, looking somewhat put out '…happens to you often?'

'Being lured to a man's house under the guise of cooking him dinner? All the time.'

'So I wasn't being in the least original?'

'Not one bit!' she said blithely.

'Bloody hell,' he murmured. 'I must be slipping. How often do you accept?'

'Very seldom,' she said seriously. 'But you did boost my ratings the last time I cooked for you so I owe you one, Mr Hunter. Besides, I'd like to use you in my next cookbook.'

He looked comically put out this time. 'As in how, Ms Belmont?'

'As in what your favourite foods are, particularly with an international flavour, including favourite little restaurants you might have around the world. You can tell me all about it while I cook.' She watched him serenely.

'So this is very definitely a quid pro quo?'

'Definitely.'

He shook his head. 'You're a hard woman, Skye. OK, I accept. Let's go.' Once more he took her hand and led her out.

For the next three months she often cooked him meals, although they never made any prior arrangements. He would simply ring her at work or at home and if she wasn't free he'd say, 'Bad luck. Maybe next time?' And she'd agree without giving any intimation that it was getting harder and harder for her to be just a good friend of Nick Hunter's.

Harder, also, to live with the thought that the last thing he would respond to was being pinned down in any way. It struck her, too, that the Skye Belmont she was presenting to Nick Hunter was her public persona, not the true girl who lurked beneath the surface and was a more serious, not-necessarily-admiring-of-the-worldliness-of-his-world girl.

Then things changed dramatically one evening. She was cooking roast beef for him. In the act of beating the ingredients for Yorkshire pudding at the same time as she was telling him about her last show, which had been a behind-the-scenes disaster, she realized he was unusually quiet.

'Am I talking too much?' she said lightly. 'I guess you had to be there to see the humour of it. Nothing came out right.'

He was sitting at the kitchen counter twirling a glass of wine in his fingers. The sun was setting, flooding his beautiful apartment and its views of Sydney Harbour with a golden radiance. And he didn't answer but only allowed his dark gaze to drift over her in a way it had once before. This time there was something darker about it, though.

She stopped beating. 'Nick—is something wrong?' she asked uncertainly.

He smiled but with an effort. 'You could say so.'

'What? Tell me?' she whispered.

'I don't know if this is on your agenda, Skye, but—even watching you make Yorkshire pudding is driving me out of my mind.'

She blinked, her mouth fell open and all she could say hoarsely was, 'Why?'

'Because I'd very much like to be kissing you.'

Several reactions hit her. Relief, disbelief and a sudden inner trembling. 'Oh. I thought it was something serious.' She stopped and blushed as he looked at her ironically. 'Well, you know what I mean—'

'No. I'm not at all sure what you mean, Skye.'

Her hands were all floury and she rubbed her forehead agitatedly, transferring some of the flour to it. 'I was thinking of an illness or... I didn't think you saw me like that. That's what I meant.'

'Then we shared the same dilemma.'

Skye sat down on a stool rather abruptly. 'Surely— I wasn't that good at covering it up?'

A fleeting frown came to his dark eyes. 'You tried to?' he hazarded.

'Oh, yes,' she said simply. 'I learnt my lesson the first time you took me to lunch.'

He got up and came round the counter so he was standing in front of her and he put his fingers beneath her chin to tilt it so he could look into her eyes. 'Didn't that put you off?' he asked sombrely, not attempting to deny the charge.

'Unfortunately, the other thing about you is that you're such fun to be with and I really enjoy your company.'

'We've never been anywhere or done anything other—than this.' He glanced around the kitchen.

She shrugged slightly.

'So—may I kiss you, Skye Belmont?'

A faint smile trembled on her lips. 'You know,

Nick, I didn't think you were the kind who waited to be asked.'

'There could be a lot of things you don't know about me, Skye,' he said, and took her in his arms.

How true, Skye thought, lying on her bed. Things that he had never intended her to get to know, either. But the sheer magic of being kissed by and intimate with Nick Hunter had claimed all her senses, including her common sense.

It had been a revelation. He'd made love to her with a mixture of laughter and intensity that had been breathtaking. Just to see his hands was enough to make her stop in her tracks and go hot and cold at the memories of how he'd handled her body, how he'd made her feel like silk and velvet, how protective his whipcord strength had been, how much pleasure he'd brought to her. How they'd laughed at the oddest things while they were lying in each other's arms.

And the way his dark gaze drifted over her, often in public, had the same effect. So that she knew he would take her to his apartment very soon, whatever they were doing, and slide her clothes off, paying meticulous attention to all her most sensitive, erogenous zones until she could barely speak. Then he'd take her to bed and their bodies would unite in a way that spoke for itself.

It struck her that if she'd once thought he was tall, dark and dangerous she now thought he was tall, dark and to die for.

Then, any hidden doubts she might have had had been allayed one day when he'd propped his head on his hand, drawn his other hand across her breasts with a touch so light yet at the same time electrifying, and said, 'I think we ought to do something to formalize this state of affairs, Ms Belmont.'

'Oh?' She'd smiled dreamily. 'Don't tell me. You're thinking of hiring me as your full-time cook?'

'On the contrary, I'm thinking of asking you to marry me.'

Skye had opened her eyes wide and sat up suddenly. 'What...?' She'd had some trouble with her voice. 'What do you mean?'

He'd eyed her quizzically. 'What do you think I mean?'

'But—' she'd groped for his hand and held it tight between hers '—I didn't know you felt like that...' She'd trailed off, and the sheer surprise had still been in her eyes.

'Skye—why do you think I keep doing this?' He'd freed his hand and pulled her into his arms. 'For that matter, *we* keep doing this,' he'd said into her hair.

She'd trembled in his arms.

'Don't tell me—' he'd raised his head and looked into her eyes quite wickedly, '—you've only been toying with me, Skye Belmont?'

Because the opposite had sometimes occurred to her, because, while it wasn't in her to toy with anyone in this way but the same might not be said of him, by reputation anyway, she'd actually gasped and looked so thunderstruck, he'd started to laugh.

'Are you serious?' she'd demanded then.

'Of course. What plans did *you* have for us?'

It was a question that had suddenly revealed all her

hidden fears to her. Fears that she hadn't been able to look in the face because his effect on her had been so powerful... Would they go on being lovers until the gloss wore off and a new woman replaced her?

How stable could a relationship be when they lived it inside a bubble—their daily lives were not in the slightest altered by it? He came and went, often with little or no explanation. She did the same, often doing the show interstate. They didn't spend much time together at all that wasn't spent in passionate lovemaking—or, it struck her with some irony, her cooking for him. Now this.

She'd looked around his bedroom and licked her lips. 'I...didn't have any plans, actually.'

'Then I think it might be time to start making them,' he'd said wryly. 'Will you marry me, Skye? I promise it's not only your cooking I love about you.'

That had done it. She'd lain back in his arms, overcome not only by him but the fact that this offer of marriage had to banish all her fears. Surely? 'Yes.' And then, in the grip of love and excitement such as she'd never known, she'd kissed him. 'Yes, please.'

That had been six months ago, she recalled. He'd bought her an engagement ring of Tanzanite, an exquisite violet blue stone that was the colour of her eyes, surrounded by diamonds. She'd met his parents and his sister and been welcomed with open arms, although she'd thought his mother had looked at her with secret surprise.

But his father had been particularly warm and welcoming of his prospective daughter-in-law, and she'd formed the impression that Richard Hunter had decided she would be good for his son.

Nick had met her mother and charmed her thoroughly. Although, again, Skye had sensed some reservations in her mother. All Iris had ever put into words, however, had been the fact that she sensed Nick Hunter might be more complicated than met the eye.

And they had become an item, Skye Belmont and Nick Hunter—a celebrity couple. Once again her ratings had skyrocketed and she'd continually had to field questions about Nick, how they'd got together, what their plans were, what the wedding would be like, her dress, the cake—would she make it herself?—their honeymoon plans, how many children they wanted.

And that, she thought sadly, lying on her bed, was when the rot had started.

Or it was the catalyst, more accurately, that had made her see she was marrying a man she adored to go to bed with, but there was not a whole lot more between them than there ever had been...

It had started out as a laughing discussion, three weeks before their wedding, on all the questions people asked her.

'While I seem to be an open book to the whole world,' she said with a grin, 'you are this mysterious figure they all hunger and thirst to know about. I can't believe people's preoccupation with you, or things like how many children we plan to have!' She grimaced.

'Well, I hope you don't plan to rush in and have an army,' he replied ruefully.

Her feeling of laughter deserted her for some reason. 'I don't intend to do either but—we are going to have kids, aren't we, Nick?'

'All in good time.'

She was cooking for him again, breakfast this time—bacon, eggs, mushrooms and tomato. She had on a yellow silk robe with nothing underneath it and all he wore was a pair of shorts. They hadn't been up long. He was reading the newspaper at the kitchen counter while she cooked.

'What do you mean, "All in good time"?'

He looked up briefly. 'You're barely twenty-four, Skye.'

'And you're thirty-two, Nick,' she countered. 'Look, I don't want to have them immediately but by the time I'm twenty-five I'm sure I shall. I will also—' she stopped, took a deep breath and looked around '—want a proper married life. I'd like my own home one day and a husband who doesn't spend half his life away from me, doing things I don't much care for anyway.'

'Such as?' He said it quietly but she divined a dangerous little glint in his eyes.

'If you must know I find your social world incredibly shallow at times. I can't stand motor racing, speedboat racing—and all the groupies who go with them—and I don't think the way you have to travel overseas so frequently is conducive to a happy life.'

'Then why are we getting married?'

'Because I thought it would change,' she said intensely. 'But I now see that out of bed we might as well inhabit different planets. Especially if you've got something against us having children!'

'I didn't say that—'

'You might just as well have, Nick; I can tell when you have reservations—about anything.'

He closed the paper at last and stood up to lean his shoulders against a cupboard. 'What is so wrong about wanting us to learn to live with each other before we set about populating the earth, Skye?'

She gasped. 'That's as good as saying you don't…you'll make your marriage vows but on the understanding you can break them!'

'It happens,' he said roughly. 'It happens to people with the best of intentions. By the way,' he added pointedly, 'I don't quibble about your work which also takes you round the country, nor have I laid down any ultimatums that you'll have to stop and devote yourself to me once we're married.'

She was speechless.

Something he took advantage of. 'As for going overseas, I'll never be able to help that. It comes with the job, but…' he paused significantly '…if you are not burdened down with babies, you could always come too.'

Shock lit her eyes. 'You really don't want kids, do you, Nick?' she whispered. 'At least tell me why?'

He stood very still for about half a minute, his dark gaze resting on her pale face. Then he said, 'Perhaps I know myself well enough to know—how hard I find it to be tied down.'

'So why—you asked me this—why *are* we getting married?'

His lips twisted. 'I hadn't figured you for such a conventional homebody, Skye.'

'Not even,' she said huskily, and put out a hand to support herself against the fridge, 'when all I've done is be at home with you?' She stared at the bacon and eggs then lifted her gaze to him. 'Could there be anything more homely than this?'

'In a sense,' he said dryly, 'that's been part of the problem. You seem so happy just to be at home.'

'So you thought you'd be able to live your old life while I stayed put and kept the home fires burning?'

'You haven't seemed to mind until now,' he pointed out.

She swallowed a great lump in her throat. 'It doesn't make sense. One moment you tell me you didn't suspect I was such a conventional home-body—'

'Ah, but that's the operative word. I didn't think you were conventional. You're very successful, Skye,' he said meditatively. 'You're very cool and confident, not at all, one would have thought, a clinger.'

'Who's talking about clinging?' she managed to say although there were tears of anger and sorrow in her eyes. 'I was talking about being in love and sharing—our lives. However, you're right in one sense. I did mislead you.'

He raised a sceptical eyebrow at her.

'Skye Belmont, as you see her on television, is not the real me. It's something I don't fully understand myself and perhaps, with you, I've extended that persona. I think I always knew when you let me dangle for two months...' She stopped and shrugged. 'Well, that I should be all cool and confident.'

'That's not how you are in bed.'

'No,' she said thoughtfully, although something felt as if it was frozen inside her—her heart? she wondered.

'Perhaps that is something we should take into account before we do anything—drastic,' he drawled.

'How good we are in bed?' She swallowed again as his dark gaze drifted down her robe, resting on the outline of her nipples beneath the thin yellow silk then the slenderness of her waist bound by the sash and finally to the curve of her hips—hips, he often told her, like perfect peaches on a slender stem. 'No, Nick,' she said hoarsely. 'For months I've...used that to...to blind myself to everything else.'

His gaze was sardonic as it reached her eyes again. 'Then what do you propose? Isn't it a little late, Skye,' he said with sudden savage impatience, 'to have this dramatic awakening? Do you know what would happen if we did go back to bed?'

She closed her eyes. 'I'm sorry but I just can't do it.'

'Sorry?' he repeated. 'You're the one with a wedding dress in your cupboard, a cake you made yourself, all your new honeymoon clothes, two bridesmaids—'

'Stop it,' she whispered, appalled. 'You're the one who has just told me you're going to resist us having children to the nth degree.'

'Skye, if it makes you happy, have them,' he said wearily.

'No, thank you, Nick. Not with you.'

'Look, this has blown out of all proportion and I can't believe you've made love to me time and time again with such *joy*—when all this was on your mind.' He raked a hand through his hair and set his teeth. 'When all these shortcomings of mine were niggling away at you!'

'Neither can I,' she said with a deadly sort of calm. 'And I *am* sorry I didn't understand and…look this in the face earlier. Goodbye, Nick.' She pulled her engagement ring off and laid it on the counter.

'Keep it,' he said dryly. 'Who knows? It might bring you some comfort when you're not in my bed, just loving it.'

Her eyes registered the sheer hurt of his words but she drew on a reserve of strength she hadn't known she possessed, and left the ring lying on the counter. 'Would you announce it? I think we'd be better doing that otherwise there'll be endless speculation.'

He laughed and picked up the ring to turn it between his long fingers. 'There's still going to be endless speculation, Skye, but if that's what you really want?'

'Yes. Thank you. I'll go now.'

His eyes captured hers. 'There's no reason we couldn't still be lovers. We're pretty good at that, whatever we may lack for marriage.'

She bit her lip to stop herself from crying out in anguish and he stood watching her attentively, the stuff her dreams were made of, until she'd run into the reality of Nick Hunter. It was as if every time they'd made love or laughed together passed before her eyes, as if she were drowning, she thought torturedly.

But remember this, she told herself. Remember his last words to you.

'Not any more,' she murmured, and turned away.

The simple announcement had been in the paper the next morning. Today, she mused. Had she hoped there would be some attempt on his part to mend things? Of course. Had she hoped a lonesome night such as she had passed last night would change him? Yes.

But no olive branch had come. Only a few formal lines on page three of the paper together with a photo of them in happier times. So it really was over and the sooner she came to grips with it, the better. Nick Hunter was not for her.

She would go away, as soon as she could arrange it. She would take the cake to a hospital and she would even donate her wedding dress to charity...

CHAPTER TWO

THREE weeks later, Skye was pounding away at a laptop computer in her bikini beside a beach so perfect, most other people would have been lost in admiration for the view.

Or lazing in the aqua shallows beside its whiteness, perhaps snorkelling over the reef with its jewel-bright coral, or simply wondering what culinary delight was in store for lunch.

Indeed, for her first few days on Haggerstone Island, way up the coast of Queensland within the Great Barrier Reef towards Cape York, Skye had done all of those things. Besides, the resort on this tropical island, with its beautiful New Guinea-style roundhouse, accommodated very few guests—part of its attraction and why she'd chosen it—and, until today, she'd been the only one.

This had suited her perfectly as she'd tried to come down from wrapping up the show for the series, and come to terms with her break-up from Nick. And the sheer beauty of the place, as well as being so far away from civilization, had helped cocoon her from her emotional turmoil.

There was nothing behind Cape Grenville, off which Haggerstone stood, but vast cattle stations. And the couple who ran the resort had literally carved it out of the wilderness themselves. So not only was it a cherished project of lovely taste and style, but the island and waters around it were home to them.

Skye had gone fishing, snorkelling and crayfish-catching with them. She was on friendly terms with Tilly, their resident wallaby, she'd sampled her hostess's marvellous cooking and spent the rest of her time relaxing in the sun or the sea.

Her fair skin was now golden, her hair was even fairer and she knew she looked healthy. It had taken the news that another guest was arriving to make her realize that her cocoon was about to split open, and to wonder about her inner health. She would more than likely be recognized and, even if she wasn't, she wanted no human contact at the moment other than the discreet, undemanding friendship she had with her hosts.

Then it had occurred to her that if she could weave Haggerstone Island and its cuisine into her book, particularly the way her hostess used a cooking pit and different grids for different effects, she not only had a legitimate reason for being too busy to socialize, she also had something wonderful to write about from a culinary point of view.

She later realized that it was impossible to be a recluse on an island with only three other people, but, most of all, quite impossible to quash Bryce Denver.

He was twenty-six, a marine biologist. He was tall but looked as if he might not have lost all his puppy fat; indeed, he was exceedingly clumsy, like an overgrown puppy—out of the water, that was. He swam like a fish. He had red hair, freckles and a shy kind of charm.

Half an hour after he'd landed on the adjacent island and been transported over the reef to Haggerstone by boat, he told Skye over lunch that he'd fallen in love with her when he'd first seen her on television and he'd breathed a sigh of absolute relief when he'd read about her breaking off her engagement to Nick Hunter...

Something about her frozen expression must have got through to him, because he slapped his forehead suddenly, knocking over his water glass in the process, and he asked her with unmistakable sorrow if she could ever forgive him for being such a callous idiot.

She assured him stiffly that she could, but made a resolve to get herself away from Haggerstone as fast as possible.

She retreated to her room after lunch. The guest accommodation was in separate cabins and hers had a superb view over the water and the reef and was cool inside with wooden shutters at the windows. She sat down and started to write furiously.

But at sunset the lure of the beach got to her and she wandered outside to watch an evening ritual she loved. The resident guinea fowl settling for the night in a magnificent coral tree in front of the roundhouse, the one peacock walking amongst the old dugout canoes planted with vivid impatiens, the quality of light over the water and beach, the beautiful serenity of Haggerstone.

She wasn't surprised when Bryce Denver came up to join her as she sat on the beach but she was surprised to find him now a gentle, amusing companion.

Perhaps it was the magic of the island that did it, she thought later. That gave him the belated tact to steer well away from anything personal, and gave her wounded psyche the balm to simply relax and go with the flow.

At any rate, she went to bed that night no longer determined to leave. Bryce was not going to be a problem, she decided. She would stay at least until she'd perfected her piece on Haggerstone.

Bryce was not a problem over the next days. As a marine biologist the waters, fish and coral around the island were the nearest thing to heaven for him. As a companion, he was rather like a younger brother despite being two years older.

He was sweet, she caught herself thinking once, and had to grimace because she knew enough about men to know he would not relish that tag. Nor might he have relinquished any dreams he'd woven around Skye Belmont, TV personality, but he was *nice* and they would be parting in a few days anyway. He to Cairns where he lived, she to Sydney.

It was the thought of Sydney that suddenly lay on her mind like a bar. The last thing she wanted to do was go home, she mused.

And that was why, in the end, when Bryce made an amazing suggestion, she agreed.

'Only one more sleep,' Bryce said regretfully over dinner, 'after tonight, that is. I believe we're flying out together?'

Skye stirred and looked rueful. 'I could stay here for ever.'

'So could I,' he agreed, 'but I've had a thought.'

Skye immediately looked wary instead of rueful.

'I'm not going straight home,' he said hastily. 'A good friend of mine has a cattle station west of Cairns and next weekend is their annual picnic race meeting. It's quite something,' he said enthusiastically. 'People come from hundreds of miles around for it and they sleep in tents, whatever—you would enjoy it, Skye.'

'Not sleeping in a tent, I wouldn't, Bryce.' She grasped the first reason she could for nipping this suggestion in the bud although she quite liked camping.

'Oh, no! I didn't mean that. My friend makes up a house party at the homestead; it's huge—the house, I mean! And he's always delighted if I bring someone with me.'

Skye sighed inwardly and reminded herself she'd known that this could be on the cards. 'Bryce, look, you've been lovely company but there couldn't ever be any more to it than that, for me.'

'Because of Nick Hunter?'

'Yes,' she said honestly.

'He must be mad!'

Skye smiled wearily. 'It was as much my fault as his but it…' She gestured. 'So I think I'm better off going home and I think you…are so *nice*, when the right girl comes along, she'll thank her lucky stars she found you.'

He grimaced.

'I mean it,' Skye said sincerely.

'I still think you should come with me. I promise not to make a nuisance of myself but it *could* make an interesting chapter for your book. They spit-roast pigs and sides of beef, they make traditional damper and billy tea, they cook witchety grubs...'

Unwittingly, Skye couldn't help looking interested.

'And there's an awful lot of colour and activity,' Bryce continued. 'Real outback stuff—calf-roping, wood-chopping contests, a boxing tent—and I'm no mean hand with a camera. I've got some lovely shots of Haggerstone for you.'

Pictures were the one thing Skye had worried about. She'd come unprepared to make a photographic diary of her sojourn. Truth to tell, although she'd brought her laptop, she hadn't seen herself as being in the frame of mind to write anything constructive.

And she knew Bryce did have an impressive array of cameras, underwater and others.

She said uncertainly, 'I'll...I'll think about it. But...'

'I always keep my promises,' Bryce said earnestly. 'Although, one day, if you ever get over him, well, who knows?'

Two days later, although she was still unsure of the wisdom of it, she flew to Cairns then on to Mount Gregory Station with Bryce Denver. He'd arranged a lift with a pilot friend of his who was flying to Weipa and who would pick them up on his return the day after the two-day race meeting.

An hour or so after they landed, she knew she had not only been unwise but quite mad, and not on account of Bryce. Nick was one of the house party. Nick with a beautiful companion in tow.

* * *

She should have suspected it when Jack Attwood, Bryce's friend, and his wife, Sally, picked them up from the station airstrip in a Land Rover. Sally did a distinct double take, then asked in an awed but also slightly anxious voice whether Skye was who she thought she was.

Bryce assured her that this was Skye Belmont but she'd rather not have any fuss made about it.

Jack greeted her warmly, and said, 'No, no, we—wouldn't dream of it. Welcome, Skye, it's a great pleasure, but…anyway.' He stopped as if unsure how to proceed, then urged them all to get into the vehicle out of the blistering sun.

On the way to the homestead, he gave them a tour of the race track with its tent population starting to swell for the two-day meeting beginning tomorrow. And he told them that this race meeting had been held on Mount Gregory since his great-grandfather's time and had become a local institution.

Skye felt a pulse of interest and excitement as she looked around. At the people, so many of them obviously outback types, at the horses, the colour, the dust, and the quaint ancient little two-tiered grandstand. It would make a perfect chapter for her book, she told Jack and Sally, if they were agreeable to her using Mount Gregory?

Sally said they would be enchanted, and they all chatted away on the drive to the homestead, with that odd little moment of anxiety forgotten, by Skye at least.

It came rushing back to her as she mounted the shallow steps to the veranda that ran around the vast old house. Afternoon tea was laid out on a long table and there were two couples enjoying it as they lounged in planter chairs.

She stopped dead as she saw who one of the men was, sitting beside a lovely girl of about her own age with a sensational figure and long dark hair, and with her hand on his arm with unmistakable familiarity. As she stopped, she heard Sally take an audible breath behind her, and Bryce tripped.

Jack broke the awful awkwardness of it in a way, he was later to confide to his wife, that was worse and definitely akin to putting his foot squarely into his mouth.

'Skye,' he said heartily, 'you probably know this bloke better than we do!'

Skye closed her eyes briefly but it was no mirage. It was Nick all right, in khaki moleskins, a red and white checked shirt, short boots, with his dark hair just the same and an unreadable expression in his eyes.

It soon fled, that expression, to give way to the look of sardonic amusement he bestowed on his friend Jack Attwood, then become almost rueful as it rested on Skye.

'Oh, dear,' he murmured, 'I left town because I'm everyone's favourite villain and—so this mightn't happen. I'm sorry, Skye, but I had no idea you were a friend of the Attwoods.'

'I'm not,' Skye heard herself say casually, and wondered where she was dredging the composure from. 'We've only just met. It was Bryce's idea.

Uh—Nick, this is Bryce Denver. Bryce—Nick Hunter.'

Don't *trip* again or knock anything over, she pleaded silently with Bryce as she introduced them.

But Bryce was perfect. He made the veranda with no further incident, held out his hand and said, 'Great to meet you, Nick! Yes, it was my idea. Skye and I have just had the most wonderful holiday on Haggerstone Island and we couldn't persuade ourselves to go home yet. So, here we are.'

If the scars within Skye hadn't been so raw and new, she would have laughed at the way Nick was momentarily floored. He went perfectly still and there was a glint of sheer disbelief in his eyes as they rested on her then flicked back to Bryce.

But instead of laughing she found herself thinking two thoughts: why shouldn't what was sauce for the gander be sauce for the goose? And had she meant so little to him, he'd waited barely a month before acquiring someone new?

But that little frozen moment broke up like a kaleidoscope pattern shifting at the end of a tube. The girl with Nick got up and introduced herself as Wynn Mortimer, and the other middle-aged couple introduced themselves as Peter and Mary Clarke, neighbours of the Attwoods.

Then they all sat down to afternoon tea.

Skye wasn't sure how she got through it but, of course, she should have known. Skye Belmont, television personality, took over. She even saw Bryce look at her once with a trace of surprise, and she realized that she'd been a somewhat muted companion during their days on Haggerstone.

Nor could she regret it, when, not long into afternoon tea, Wynn displayed a high-powered personality. She was funny, she was extremely articulate as well as obviously sophisticated. She talked about her recent trip to Africa on a modelling assignment and had them all in stitches when she described a close encounter with five white rhino. She also revealed she was a champion water-skier.

Just what he needs, Skye caught herself thinking cynically. Not someone who would love to cook for him, by the sound of it. Or ruin her figure bearing his children. At that moment, she happened to encounter Nick Hunter's dark eyes on her.

She felt a frisson run through her as he made no attempt to hurry his inspection of her denim pinafore shorts over a lovely dotted white voile blouse. Or her sun-lightened hair and golden skin, and her legs down to the pair of white sand shoes she wore.

'You're looking well, Skye,' he said then, into a lull in the conversation.

'Thank you,' she responded, trying to sound carefree and then determined to mean it. 'So are you. I wonder what that means?' she added with an imp of mischief dancing in her eyes.

'That we broke it off in the nick of time?' he drawled.

Conscious of the rest of the company holding their breath in a manner of speaking, plus quite unable to rein in the devil that was riding her, she laughed. 'I think you might be right. Please don't feel embar-

rassed,' she said to everyone at large. 'It is over between Nick and me, but I'm sure we can be civilized
about it. Possibly even friends?' She turned back to
him with the question in her eyes.

'I don't see why not, Skye,' he said after a moment,
and turned to Bryce. 'Tell me about yourself, mate.
As a friend I'd still like to know she's in good hands.'

She should have known, Skye thought, trembling
inwardly, that taking on Nick was asking for trouble,
but once again Bryce came to the rescue.

'I fell in love with Skye when I first saw her on
television,' he said simply. He smiled placidly at
Nick. 'Do you want to know what my prospects and
background are? I'd be happy to tell you.'

Sally rose. 'Well, while you do that, Bryce, I'm
going to show the girls their rooms. Dinner is at
seven—goodness me, it's five o'clock already! You
might like to have a little rest...'

The room Skye was shown to was comfortable in an
old-fashioned way and had its own bathroom. And
Sally Attwood, who was a good hostess as well as
kind-hearted, decided to take the bull by the horns as
she showed Skye round it.

'I'm so sorry about this,' she said anxiously.
'We've always told Bryce, and Nick for that matter,
that if they'd like to bring someone—don't even ask,
just do it! Now—' She broke off and shrugged.
'You've found yourself in this awful situation. Unless
you and Bryce *are*...?' She looked a question at Skye.

Skye sank down in a comfortable armchair, feeling
suddenly exhausted. 'No.' And she explained exactly

how it had happened. 'I shouldn't have done it, though,' she went on. 'It's not fair to him and now I've fallen into the trap of *using* him in a sort of...well, horrible tit-for-tat game with Nick.'

Sally sat down on the end of the bed to say thoughtfully, 'There's more to Bryce than appears on the surface, Skye. I think he can probably take care of himself. But would I be right in thinking you haven't entirely got over Nick Hunter?'

Realization that she was confiding in a complete stranger came belatedly to Skye. But there was something so warm and concerned in the other woman's eyes, she smiled wearily. 'You'd be right. I just hope to heaven I wasn't as transparent to everyone else!'

'You were wonderful, just like the girl on television,' Sally said enthusiastically.

Ah, Skye thought. Did anyone have an inkling that she might be developing a split personality?

Sally went on before she could say anything. 'I just, well, it must all be so new—that's what made me wonder.'

Skye sat up. 'I think it might be easier for everyone if I go home, Sally. I...well, it's got to be uncomfortable for others to be caught in this kind of crossfire and I'd hate myself for turning your big weekend into a disaster. Is there...how would I go about it?'

Sally Attwood looked into those amazing though shadowed blue eyes. Then she took a deep breath, and said, 'Don't go, Skye. I don't know what went wrong but once you run away from Nick you'll find yourself doing it all the time. And don't worry about us! There's going to be enough on over the next two days for us to find plenty of cover.' She grinned then sobered. 'Please?'

'Well…'

'Good girl.' Sally rose. 'By the way, we dress for dinner but nothing too formal. We'll have a pre-dinner drink in the lounge at about half past six. See you there!' And she was gone, leaving Skye staring bemusedly at the door.

A long soak in the tub did much for Skye's morale. Not only did the lovely warm water combined with her fragrant bath oil help, but so did the growing conviction that Sally was right. She couldn't spend her life running away from Nick. Because she *was* liable to run into him again, and the sooner she incised the hurt of their parting the better. This might just be the way to do it—with a show of strength now.

She chose a knee-length, shoe-string strap, pale grey dress in a fine silk knit that clung to her figure, to wear to dinner. It was a dress she loved because it packed wonderfully, was very versatile—and it was the only dressy dress she'd brought. She teamed it with a chunky, gorgeous silver and turquoise bangle, silver sandals and a turquoise slide in her hair.

And she left her room with her skin smooth and glowing, her hair shining and curly, and feeling chic and ready to take on the world. But despite the fact that it was already a quarter to seven only Nick was in the lounge with a drink in his hands.

'Oh.' She hovered in the doorway.

He turned. 'As you say, Skye,' he murmured, and a glint of mockery flew her way from his dark eyes.

He wore beige corduroy trousers, a long-sleeved cream shirt and a dark red tie.

She gritted her teeth and walked into the room. 'Where is everyone?'

'I have no idea, apart from Wynn, who is wrestling with what to wear tonight. Unlike you—' his gaze skimmed the dress he knew well '—she doesn't travel light.' His dark eyes came back to rest on her face enigmatically.

Skye flinched and looked away. It had been a joke they'd shared that she was one of the few women he knew who did. In fact she'd almost made it an art form because she did spend a lot of time on the road with the show.

The other thing that had caused her to flinch, however, was the way he could still undress her with his eyes. How dared he? she wondered hotly. Did he think she couldn't read what was behind that enigmatic glance? Why would he anyway...?

'Talking of that,' she said after a long moment during which she fought for cool composure, 'they're thinking of including a segment on how to travel light in the next series. Perhaps—' a little glint of humour lit her eyes '—I could give Wynn a few tips?'

He smiled faintly. 'I wish you would. I don't imagine it would endear you to her, however. What would you like to drink? The same?'

She stopped herself from wincing visibly this time. 'Yes, thank you.'

He poured her a gin and tonic and brought it over to her. 'Do sit down, Skye,' he invited, this time with a sardonic little glint.

She accepted the glass and sank down on a settee. Jack and Sally's lounge was, like the rest of the house, done on a grand scale. The chintz-covered chairs and settees were plump and vast. So much so that she immediately felt as if she was stranded on an island.

She raised an eyebrow wryly, and looked around at the paintings on the old wooden walls, the massive pieces of mahogany and cedar furniture, the parchment lampshades, the pot plants in old brass containers. There were French doors that opened onto the veranda, and a dark velvet sky beyond.

Nick seated himself opposite her, and looked around too. 'It was all built to last,' he commented.

Skye sipped her drink. 'How long have you known them?'

'Years,' he said lazily. 'I often come up here for some R and R.'

Skye opened her mouth to ask why he'd never mentioned them to her or brought her here, then closed it abruptly.

'You were always doing something else,' he said with soft but deadly satire.

A tinge of colour ran through her cheeks at the way he'd read her mind so accurately. But she decided not to respond. She simply shrugged instead.

'Where did you pick up Bryce Denver?' he asked then.

Skye put her glass down carefully on an occasional table. 'I didn't pick him up. It was the other way around if anything, but—' she gazed at him, her eyes a deep and furious blue '—talking of such things, where did you pick up Wynn?'

'Well, not that I'm complaining,' he drawled, 'but it was also the other way around if anything.'

The parody on her words further incensed her. Then she remembered her fighting words to herself about a show of strength, and she thought briefly.

'Nick,' she said finally, 'it doesn't matter where or how you and Wynn got together. The same goes for Bryce but—there's nothing between us. We just happened to meet on Haggerstone and when he suggested Mount Gregory as a good setting for a chapter in my book I agreed.'

'So he didn't fall in love with you as soon as he saw you on television?'

'He—you know how unrealistic that is, or maybe you don't,' she said barely audibly, 'but—'

'And you don't think the *reality* of Skye Belmont has caused him to fall even harder for you?' he overrode her cynically.

'It... I...' She drew a breath. 'It's got nothing to do with you, Nick.'

'So why are you telling me all this?' he asked dryly.

'I'm telling you because I don't intend to play games, or hide behind Bryce because *you've* got yourself a girlfriend—and it's not fair to him anyway.'

'Perhaps you should be telling Bryce this,' he murmured.

'I have! He...' She paused frustratedly and Nick started to laugh softly.

'Continues to live in hope?'

Skye pressed her lips together.

'Tell me something else, then,' he said, narrowing his eyes. 'What have you got against him?'

'Nothing. I…like him very much. I'm just not prepared to…' She paused.

'Get yourself misunderstood by another man?' he suggested with irony.

'Precisely.' She stared at him challengingly. But at that moment Wynn drifted into the room, looking extremely sexy in an outfit she appeared to have been poured into. An all-in-one lime-green trouser suit with a halter top—under which she clearly wore no bra.

'Well, well,' she purred, 'going over old times, you two? I hope you're not having second thoughts, Skye,' she added, and didn't have to say the obvious as she strolled over to Nick with her fluid, model's walk, and put her arm through his in a way that shouted, The man is mine!

Her sense of humour came to Skye's rescue. 'No, but if you'd like any tips on how to handle the man— I'm sure I could give you a few. That is a sensational outfit, Wynn. Did you wear it in Africa? Maybe not; you might have caused a riot.' She eyed Wynn innocently but with obvious laughter in her eyes.

For an instant, there was all the tension of a riot brewing in Jack and Sally's lounge, as Wynn's lovely face contorted, but Bryce arrived on the scene, followed by the Clarkes, and hot on their heels came Jack and Sally, full of apologies for being so late.

Skye took the moment to reflect that she hated being bitchy although she had genuinely been moved to laughter, but on this occasion it had felt wonderful!

She blinked, in some surprise, and looked up to see Nick watching her as everyone else milled around the cocktail cabinet.

Had he read her mind again? she wondered. If so, why was there something unusually thoughtful in that dark gaze? As if he was puzzled... Hadn't he expected her to be able to defend herself against Wynn? she wondered, and moved her slim shoulders in slight perplexity.

To her amazement, he smiled briefly, and raised his glass to her. Then Bryce came to sit beside her and the moment was lost.

Dinner was enormous.

A delicious zucchini soup, followed by fillets of whiting then roast pork with all the accompaniments: potatoes, pumpkin, cauliflower *au gratin*, apple sauce and gravy. The dessert was poached pears and a cheeseboard followed.

When Skye commented that it had been absolutely delicious, Sally looked gratified and said that having Skye Belmont in one's house sure put one on one's mettle!

Wynn, who had eaten less than any one, contrived to look bored. It was something she managed to do every time any mention of Skye's fame was made.

Afterwards, the Attwoods pursued what was obviously a time-honoured tradition. They rolled back a rug in the lounge, put some music on the CD player and, with some hilarity, started to dance.

'I'd forgotten about this,' Bryce said gloomily as everyone took up their partners.

Truth to tell, Skye was not enamoured of the idea either but she said, 'It's probably a good idea after a meal like that.'

'Yes, but I bet you don't have two left feet,' he commented, looking gloomier than ever.

'Ah... Has anyone ever tried to show you how?'

'Some have tried. All have failed. I just don't seem to have any rhythm as well as being so clumsy.'

'Bryce, trust me.' All of a sudden Skye found herself forgetting her problems in the face of his genuine look of deep apprehension as he stood in front of her. 'Tell you what, forget about any conventional steps; those days are long gone. All you have to do is your own thing. And I have seen you weave your way through the water with a rhythm of a kind that was quite magical.'

'I'm never the same on dry land.'

'Just think the music into the swirl of the sea. Like this.' She took his hand and began to sway gently herself, using her other hand as a mermaid might trail her fingers through the water. It was a soft, dreamy piece of music.

Half an hour later they'd swirled their way through much livelier waters and Bryce had started to cotton on, even become quite inventive. And Skye had almost been able to wrest her mind from the awful impact of seeing another woman in Nick's arms. Nor was Wynn a discreet dancer. She took a—malicious? Skye wondered—pleasure in displaying her undeniably sensational figure in a variety of poses. She was graceful and sinuous and she wound herself around Nick time and time again.

Then disaster struck. So amazed was Bryce, as she got him to relax and co-ordinate his body to the music, he pulled her into his arms and kissed her enthusiastically. 'You're a genius, Skye. And you're so nice! He must be crazy to have broken up with you—'

The silence was crashing although the music played on. Everyone stopped dancing and Bryce came crashing back to earth, literally, as his feet got all tangled up and his face flamed.

'He's OK.'

It was Nick, for some reason, who delivered the news to Skye as she sat on the darkened veranda outside her room.

'He's sprained his ankle, that's all, and not that seriously. Jack's got a support bandage and he'll be able to hobble around with a stick tomorrow.'

Two tears slid down Skye's cheeks. In the mêlée that had followed Bryce's crash to the floor, in his awful embarrassment and everyone else's, she'd suddenly found herself unable to cope with this day any longer, and had retreated to her room while Jack, Nick and Peter had hoisted Bryce to his feet and tried to assess the damage.

'He was so thrilled,' she whispered, licking the salt from her lips.

Nick sat down beside her on the wooden bench.

'He'll get over it.'

'You don't understand. You have no idea what it's like to be shy and dysfunctional. Everything comes naturally to you.'

'You say that quite bitterly, Skye, but a lot of things come naturally to you.'

She sighed. 'They may do on television; they come with great difficulty at other times.'

'What do you mean?' He frowned.

'Nothing,' she said hastily. 'I—'

'But I would hardly call you dysfunctional, Skye.' He overrode her, still with that frown.

She bit her lip then paused to reflect that if she hadn't been able to confide in him about a certain problem she'd discovered she had about her face being so instantly recognisable when they were engaged, nor had he ever guessed there was a problem, why should she have it dragged out of her now?

'Of course I'm not dysfunctional,' she said, 'but I do know what it's like to be shy and to be inherently clumsy has got to be a handicap. So, yes, I sympathise with him, that's all.' She stopped then went on with feeling, 'If I'd had any sense, I'd never have come here. And not *only* because of you.'

'Point taken,' he replied evenly. 'But in the face of such devotion I don't think you should discount Bryce—'

'Nick—' she shook her head wearily '—don't tell me who I should discount or otherwise.'

'Even when you're sitting here in tears over him?'

'That's…well, I told you! You'd have to have a heart of stone not to feel for him! Besides, I'm tired and emotional. It hasn't been the easiest of days.'

He was silent for a time.

Until Skye said, 'Why did they send *you* to tell me this?'

'They didn't. They all thought you'd gone to bed. I just happened to decide I needed a bit of fresh air.'

'Well, you better take it and get back before Wynn comes to look for you.'

He laughed softly. 'You certainly put a shot across her bows before dinner, Skye.'

Skye turned to him with a frown. 'Don't you mind?'

'Mind what?'

'That I don't think much of your latest choice in women, Nick,' she said deliberately.

'To be honest, Skye, I wouldn't have expected you to like whomever I had with me.'

Skye stood up abruptly. 'Because you imagine I regret breaking off our engagement?'

'Because one minute you were sleeping with me and cooking me breakfast, and virtually the next minute you'd gone? Oh, yes,' he said, 'I think there has to be some regret, otherwise it just doesn't make sense.'

Skye wandered over to the veranda railing and studied the stars.

'Do you remember one night when we had my parents' place all to ourselves, for example?' he went on.

She stiffened and refused to turn to him.

'Do you remember taking a midnight swim in the pool? In the nude?'

'Nick—'

'Not that you were entirely nude. If I remember correctly, you had on a pair of daring little G-string panties—daring for you because I don't think you'd ever worn them before. All the same you were exquisite in the moonlight with drops running off your breasts when I lifted you out of the water, with your skin sleek, your body so slim yet curved in all the right places.'

Skye closed her eyes and fought the memories but it was useless. How to forget the feel of his hands on her as he'd lifted her from the water that night and held her up? Or forget how a little breeze on her wet skin had caused her nipples to unfurl, how she'd twined her legs around his waist and wrapped her arms around his neck and how wonderful the close contact of their cool, wet bodies had been...?

'We didn't make it back to the house,' he mused reminiscently. 'It was a magnificent night and we found a patch of lawn under a tree, but at first you weren't all that keen, despite how we'd frolicked in the pool. You looked at me as if to say, This is living just a bit *too* dangerously, Nick. So we sat wrapped in our towels, I built a fire out of leaves and twigs, and we held hands and told each other jokes until we couldn't stop laughing.'

Skye gritted her teeth and knew it was no good asking him what he thought he was doing. Because she knew only too well—he was reminding her of exactly what she'd walked away from. Although why he was choosing to do it was another matter—male ego? Surely Wynn would have restored that by now...

'Then you didn't seem to mind making...' he paused '...lovely, exciting love to me under that tree, Skye.'

She turned slowly at last. 'I remember. I wasn't

even that keen on swimming in the nude to start with. So if you're trying to say you liberated me from some of my inhibitions, so you did.' She swallowed.

'And that's something you regret?' His gaze was terribly mocking.

She folded her arms as she leant back against a post, and forced herself to say quietly, 'What I do regret is not knowing how much of it was the real me or the other Skye Belmont who thought she was doing the things Nick Hunter wanted her to do.'

'That's crazy—'

'That's not so crazy, Nick,' she said steadily. 'But of course there are other regrets. You're...wonderful to sleep with, lovely company and all the rest, but you're not for me.'

There was silence then she straightened, walked over to him and put the tips of her fingers on his cheek, and went on, 'So, don't take any notice of what I might think about Wynn. Because she'll suit you far better than I would have. Goodnight.'

She disappeared into her room like a wraith in the night.

Nick Hunter swore beneath his breath.

CHAPTER THREE

SKYE slept dreamlessly and woke early.

But as she lay in bed and listened to a rooster crowing her conversation with Nick came back to her vividly. And the thought slid into her mind that she should be on television... It had been that kind of bravura performance she'd put on after he'd done his damnedest to make her ache with desire for him.

Of course, she was on television, she reminded herself ironically. That was half the problem. But a new problem was raising its head within her. Since when had she taken to deluding herself?

Because, at the time, she'd meant every word she'd said to Nick. Yet the truth was she bitterly regretted losing him; she felt as if she'd been torn in two; life without him was almost unbearable. But, worse than that, the thought of him with another woman was a form of torture. Especially a woman she could put a name and a face to—a woman like Wynn Mortimer. Just to watch them dancing together had been hell...

She must be mad, she thought miserably as she lay against a vast feather pillow in her blue silk nightgown with her hands folded upon a white crocheted coverlet.

So what did that translate to? That she'd been mad to break up with Nick in the first place? That the

56

defences and the arguments she'd put up at the time
had been trivial?

'No,' she said aloud and softly, with a frown of
pain. 'And more so now because he made no effort
to understand or come to a compromise, and whether
she picked him up or not he's still with someone
else!'

Which brought Bryce to mind, and she sighed
heavily. How on earth had she got herself into this
terrible predicament? What could she do?

Go home, a little voice said in her head. She cast
aside the bedclothes, full of sudden decision.

Almost everyone had other ideas, however.

Bryce was the first person she encountered.

Breakfast was laid out on the table on the veranda
and he was sitting at the table with a walking stick
beside him and his bound ankle resting on a cushion
on the floor.

'Bryce,' she said warmly, 'how are you?'

He raised his eyes to hers slowly. 'Wishing there
was an almighty hole I could crawl into,' he replied
with great feeling.

'Don't—please don't feel like that,' she pleaded.
'It was the kind of accident that could have happened
to anyone.'

'You don't really believe that, Skye,' he said
gloomily. 'And it wasn't only what I did but what I
said! I'm sure that's why you ran away,' he added,
with a suddenly acute little look.

Skye grimaced and sat down beside him. 'To be

honest, Bryce, there was nothing I could think of to say or do—it just…'

'Was the last straw?' he supplied.

She shrugged. 'It wasn't an easy day.'

'Don't I know it? I'm just hoping and praying you're not thinking of going home because of it?'

Skye poured herself some orange juice as she tried to marshal the right words to say. 'Well, since you mention it—'

Bryce sat up urgently. '*Don't*, Skye. You'll never get over him if you keep running away from him.'

'That's what Sally said but I feel like a—I just *know* I shouldn't be here. Dear Bryce,' she added contritely, 'I'm truly sorry; you've been so sweet—'

'Then why don't you leave him to the machinations of that awful woman and just take a bit of time to get to know me better, Skye?'

Skye blinked several times and several expressions chased across her face. 'So you don't like her either?' she said, and immediately wondered why she was taking up the least important point of his surprising statement. 'I mean—it doesn't matter, of course, but—'

'No, I don't. I never have liked that kind of man-eating woman.'

For a moment Skye was tempted to burst out laughing, so distasteful did he look. But he then took her breath away by adding, 'I would also like the question of Nick Hunter finally resolved for you, Skye, because—and please don't feel you have to take the least responsibility for this—then you might just *want* to get to know me better.'

'Oh, Bryce,' she said on a sigh, 'I was afraid of this, but look…' She paused and frowned.

That was when Mary Clarke joined them on the veranda and after they'd exchanged greetings and she'd asked after Bryce's ankle she said diffidently to Skye, 'I've sent Peter home, Skye, to pick up my grandmother's cookbook. It's an absolute gem of a country woman's cookbook and she illustrated it herself in the margins. You're very welcome to use any of the recipes in your book.'

'Home?' Skye said. 'I thought—'

'That's a drive of about a hundred miles,' Bryce contributed.

'He won't mind that. He's used to driving long distances,' Mary said serenely. 'We could go through it together sometime today or tomorrow. I know you'll be fascinated.'

Skye swallowed. 'That's really kind of you, Mary. Thank you very much. I…I…'

It was Jack who arrived on the veranda this time, to put a further dampener on Skye's plans to go home. Jack flew his own plane and it wouldn't have taken long for him to fly her to Cooktown where there were commercial flights to Cairns. Jack, however, arrived scratching his head and muttering about fuel injectors. Nick was with him and they'd both obviously scrubbed up for the meal but still had grease streaks on their clothes.

It was Bryce who sat up suddenly and said on a note of eagerness unbefitting the situation, 'Don't tell me you're earthbound at the moment, Jack?'

'Sure am. I'll have to get a part flown in from Cairns but the earliest they can do it is Monday.'

Skye concealed a sigh of sheer frustration and asked herself what the alternative was. A long, back-breaking lift in a vehicle with a stranger? Trouble was, all roads were leading *to* Mount Gregory at the moment. And that only left Nick, who, despite being engaged to her for six months, had never flown her anywhere, which was why she hadn't recognized his light plane on the station strip.

How could she ask him to fly her out?

Wynn set the seal on her fate by arriving last at breakfast, and completely ignoring her.

Don't take offence, Skye warned herself. Don't take—anything! But she did. She suddenly found herself determined to stay on—a determination that had nothing to do with the fact that she had little choice.

The rest of breakfast was spent discussing plans for the day. They'd have an early light lunch, Sally suggested, then hit the race track. But if anyone wanted to wander down beforehand and see the sights they should please feel free to do so.

Skye decided to do exactly that, on her own, with a notebook and pencil.

It required being less than honest and open to achieve it, however. As soon as she saw Bryce gearing himself to accompany her should she desire to go walkabout, she murmured something about spending an hour with her laptop, to put her initial impressions of Mount Gregory down. Jack then suggested he drive Bryce and whoever was interested to see a new stud bull he'd acquired.

But in the seclusion of her room Skye didn't even open her laptop. She put on a pair of khaki trousers, a checked shirt that she left hanging out, and boots. She flattened her hair to her head and put on a straight brown wig with a long fringe and added a battered felt broad-brimmed cattleman's hat that she'd borrowed from the stand in the hall. As a final precaution, she donned a pair of wrap-around, very dark sunglasses.

And, confident that no one would recognize her, she slipped out the back way.

No one did recognize her and for at least an hour she wandered around the tent city that had grown beside the race track. It was fascinating.

Mount Gregory was a huge cattle station, most of it rolling scrub country, criss-crossed by cattle trails in the red earth. It was isolated, prone to droughts and floods, and it was often awesomely beautiful, as Jack had been describing to them over dinner the previous evening. When its billabongs were full of bird life, when a good season brought tiny wild flowers, when the colours of the country took your breath away— red ochre, sage-green, blue sky.

But it was a hard life living and working in this country. And its people loved a chance to party. As they gave every indication of as Skye wandered around.

There were hot-food stalls, gambling games, people selling leather goods like belts and stock whips, as well as semiprecious stones. She caught herself thinking that Nick would be interested.

There were huge dogs tied up in the back of small

trucks, plenty of evidence of a good, solid intake of beer and very much a carnival atmosphere. There were horses everywhere, as well as broad-brimmed, high-crowned felt hats such as the one she was wearing.

It was the beer intake that nearly brought about her undoing. A tall man with a slurred voice and a very red face started to follow her, making comments about what a nice little heifer she looked to be. She ignored him but decided it might be time to head back to the homestead.

Her admirer had other ideas. He came up and tried to put his arms around her, breathing beery fumes all over her as she struggled to get free. The next moment he was lying in the dust and she was clamped to someone else's chest.

Someone who said, 'Skye, should you be wandering around on your own?'

Her heart, already beating heavily from the encounter with the drunk, began to beat a different tattoo because these arms and this chest felt so much like home to her.

'Nick,' she gasped gratefully. Then, as it occurred to her that, by her own hand, she'd given up all rights to this kind of intimacy with Nick Hunter, she said a little desperately, 'Let me go, Nick. I'm fine.'

He let her go.

'How…how did you know it was me?' she stammered.

That dark gaze drifted wryly down her in a manner she knew so well, pausing quizzically on her brown hair then continuing leisurely. 'The way you walk,' he said softly, 'your hands, your—outline, which I happen to know rather well.'

Her face flamed.

'But is a wig really necessary?' he went on, touching a tress of the brown hair that lay on her shoulder.

'You never know,' she said stiffly. 'Um...I just wanted to get some of the local colour. For my book. On my own.'

He took her hand and led her through a gate into a grassed area behind the old grandstand. 'You succeeded,' he drawled. 'You should have taken into account that even incognito you present a very tempting—outline, Skye.'

'Were you following me?' she asked tartly; it was all she could think of to say.

'I didn't set out to but once I realized it was you, yes. The other thing you should have thought of, Skye, is that a lot of the men here lead lonely, women-less lives on huge cattle stations.'

'I...' She paused awkwardly. 'Well, I didn't stop to think about that,' she confessed. 'But anyway—I thought you, and everyone else, had gone to see the bull.'

'So we did. I thought *you* were going to work on your book.'

'I am. In a way—All right, I lied,' she confessed. 'It was Bryce I was...' She stopped.

'Trying to evade?' he queried.

Skye sighed. 'Yes. But as much on account of his ankle as anything else. What *are* you doing down here?'

He produced a key and unlocked a door that led

into a little room under the stand. 'For my sins I'm an honorary steward today. Come in.'

Skye followed him in and looked around. There was a large scale, a table and hard chairs and not much else.

'This does duty as the weigh-in area for the jockeys and the steward's room,' he explained. 'It is now my task to write the final scratchings from each race on the blackboards on the wall outside.' He pulled a sheaf of papers from the pocket of his jeans. 'There are a lot of them,' he added dryly.

'Would you have two pieces of chalk?'

'Are you proposing to help me, Skye?' he asked with a glint of irony.

'Why not?'

'After the shots we fired at each other last night it does seem a little surprising.' His gaze was steady on her face.

She shrugged. 'Since then you've saved me from a fate worse than death, and since *everybody*,' she said bitterly, 'has conspired against all my plans to leave Mount Gregory so that you're stuck with me, Nick, why not?'

He sat down on the corner of the table and studied her narrowly. 'Last night you appeared to have no problem about being stuck here with *me*, Skye.'

'Maybe not,' she said after a quick think, 'but Bryce is another matter.'

'Ah.' He folded his arms. 'By the way, I didn't conspire against you because I didn't know your plans.'

'You're the last person I could ask to fly me out,' Skye said prosaically.

'Why?'

She looked at him frustratedly. 'You must see why!'

'No, I don't.'

'Because it's tantamount to admitting that I'm…running away from you—' She broke off and bit her lip.

'However you went and whoever you went with, it would still have the same connotations,' he pointed out.

'Perhaps,' Skye conceded through her teeth, 'but— Oh, this is ridiculous! Anyway, much as it irks me to admit this, and I'm not admitting anything else, Nick…' she warned, and stopped.

'No?' He raised a lazy eyebrow at her.

'No. You're the one who just can't see how… impossible it would be to ask you of all people to fly me out!'

'I'm still a bit puzzled,' he murmured, 'but go on. Something else irks you?'

She paused and eyed him crossly. Then she grimaced inwardly as she wished devoutly she'd never got herself into this, and tried for another approach. 'This is going to sound really feminine and illogical, Nick, but, since you never, ever flew me anywhere despite being engaged to me and all the rest, I have no intention of starting to fly with you now.' She even managed to look casually quizzical as she said it.

He laughed softly.

Skye went on before he could say anything, though.

'No, that pleasure is entirely Wynn's now! Do you want me to help you chalk up scratchings, Nick Hunter, or not? I'm getting tired of this kind of...' She gestured impatiently.

'Chit-chat? You're right, we don't seem to be making much sense, so—' he stood up '—yes, please, Skye Belmont; if you'd like to help I'd be happy to have it.'

The 'much sense' bit made her look annoyed but what he said then was worse.

'On second thoughts, I wouldn't have flown you out, you know. Because I think Bryce deserves another chance. Here's your chalk. I'll do the first four races, you can do the last four. After you.'

He handed her a piece of chalk and stood aside for her to precede him out into the sunlight.

Skye closed her mouth, ignored the glint of satire in his dark eyes and stalked outside.

Lunch was cold meat and salad, ice cream and fruit salad accompanied by tea and coffee.

Sally told them that champagne and snacks would be available in a tent that had been erected for their use as well as other friends of the Attwoods down at the course. And, having earlier imparted the news that she intended to dress up and wear a hat, she lent one to Skye, the only one who had come hatless, except for a floppy linen sunhat.

Of the four hats she'd had to choose from, Skye had selected a delightful black tulle confection with a wide, down-turned brim. It was a good sort of camouflage hat and not a curl of her trademark hair showed beneath it. With her sunglasses on, she thought that she again might be unrecognizable. She teamed it with a sleeveless black figure-hugging knit shirt, black trousers and a big silk yellow rose pinned to the waistband of her trousers.

As she dressed with care after lunch, she realized she was trying to blank out her last encounter with Nick. Because, to her horror, just to think of it brought tears to her eyes. And her mother's words of wisdom on the subject of Nick Hunter—that he might be more complicated than appeared on the surface— came back to mind.

But what was so complicated about him? she wondered sadly. He had certainly adjusted to parting from her with what looked like amazing ease. He surely couldn't be pushing her towards Bryce otherwise, not to mention his relationship with her nemesis, Wynn Mortimer. So, if there was anything deep, dark and complicated about him, she had never touched it.

She stared at herself in the mirror, closed her eyes briefly then adjusted her hat—and went to the races.

Several hours later, she came back from the races, tossed her hat onto the bed, slipped her shoes off and sank into the armchair. It had been a fun afternoon. She'd backed a couple of winners, consumed some champagne, watched the antics of the crowd with amusement and looked after Bryce admirably.

Inasmuch as when he'd tired of hobbling around on his sprained ankle, between the mounting yard, the bookmakers and the grandstand, she'd procured a couple of folding chairs for them in the family tent.

And she'd brought him champagne and food, taken his commissions to the bookmakers and come back to describe each race to him.

Yes, she thought tiredly, laying her head back, Skye Belmont, TV personality, had been at her bubbly best. Even Wynn Mortimer, stunning in a white leather miniskirt and matching sleeveless, low-cut top teamed with a ruby-red cartwheel hat crowned with feathers, had failed to render her less than bubbly. The fact that Nick, due to the weight of his honorary steward duties, was not much in evidence had also helped.

To make matters worse, another bravura performance was required of her tonight. The Owners and Trainers Ball was being held in a large marquee and the Attwood house party made a practice of attending.

'I didn't bring anything to wear to a ball!' she'd protested when apprised of this. 'Anyway, I'm sure Bryce isn't up to it.'

Bryce had expressed the opinion that, whilst he wouldn't be up to dancing and might never attempt to do so again, he would still go. *Please come, Skye, they'd all entreated. It's part of the Mount Gregory experience; you can't miss it and we don't really dress up for a ball!* All bar two, that was.

Nick had simply watched her impassively while Wynn had turned her back on the proceedings.

She'd agreed reluctantly and Sally had offered to lend her something to wear which she'd declined, saying she'd come up with something herself.

Nick had spoken for the first time. 'I'm sure you will, Skye—you're good at that. I think Skye must have the smallest wardrobe of any woman I've known but she always manages to make it exciting.'

Skye's eyes had blazed at him before she too had turned her back on the proceedings.

'I don't think I can take much more,' she murmured to herself in the privacy of her bedroom. 'And I refuse to be bubbly tonight! So take heed, Skye Belmont.' She went to take a bath.

'Nick was right. You look stunning. And you always manage to look different, somehow.'

Skye glanced down at herself then up at Bryce. She wore the same outfit as she had to the races. But the rose was gone, she'd exchanged her black patent shoes for her silver high-heeled sandals and she'd added a marvellous pale grey shawl with black and turquoise flowers on it. She wore it over one shoulder and tied at her waist on the opposite side. Her hair was pulled severely back in a knot.

'Nick was not trying to be right,' she murmured. 'He was trying to lump me in with all the other women he has known. No doubt a multitude.'

'Was that the reason you broke it off with him?'

They were walking slowly towards the ball marquee, having fallen behind the rest of the party as Bryce hobbled along. There was another dark, velvety sky above them, pricked by a million stars, and there was the aroma of wood smoke and meat cooking on the air, coming from glowing camp fires dotted around. Not everyone had been fortunate enough to be invited to the Owners and Trainers Ball.

Or were they *more* fortunate than she was? Skye

mused. She had no doubt many a party was being held out in the open and for a moment she longed to break free and go and find herself one.

'Skye?'

'Uh.' She wrested her mind back to what Bryce had said. 'No, as a matter of fact. Well, not any that I knew about.'

'So what was the problem?'

Skye sighed. 'He wasn't who I thought he was and I definitely was not the kind of wife he…wanted.'

'Then it was a very close shave,' Bryce said with a frown.

'You're not wrong. Bryce, I'm not really looking forward to this so, if you feel like leaving early, please tell me!'

He took her hand. 'Trust me, Skye. You'll end up enjoying yourself!'

It was hard not to.

The band might have been a country band but they were innovative and lively and the lead singer was a fair Elvis Presley impersonator. Everyone danced with everyone else, although Skye managed to avoid Nick, or, it struck her, perhaps it was the other way around? And the Clarks' nineteen-year-old daughter, Maggie, arrived unexpectedly, sporting a broken arm.

This turned out to be ideal for Bryce, who had met her years ago, because she kept him company, saying that any energetic movement was painful so she wouldn't be dancing.

Apparently she'd fallen off a boat unbeknownst to her parents, who'd believed she was safe and sound at the James Cook University in Townsville, industriously studying marine biology.

As soon as Skye heard about the marine biology, she recalled the look of surprise in Bryce's eyes on being presented with a nineteen-year-old Maggie Clarke who obviously differed greatly from his memories of her. She was short but slender, dark and elfin and, although not precisely beautiful, she had lovely large brown eyes that sparkled with fun.

Could this be the answer to one set of her prayers? Skye asked herself. What could be more perfect for tearing Bryce's infatuation away from her than an attractive, soon-to-be marine biologist with a broken arm? The other plus for Maggie was that she did not come across as a man-eater, just a happy, friendly girl.

It was this set of thoughts that caused Skye to suddenly feel more in tune with the Owners and Trainers Ball. Also, there was such a crowd, it was quite easy to lose sight of Nick and Wynn.

It was while she was dancing with Jack Attwood that she said suddenly, though, 'I'd love to know what they're cooking on those camp fires, and not only for my book. I mean—' she looked contrite '—this is fun, but the real Mount Gregory atmosphere is out there, would I be right in thinking?'

Jack grinned. 'Between you and me, Skye, that's where I'd rather be but Sally insists we grace the ball. Uh...' he paused and looked around.'.. 'I'd get skinned alive if I left but, look, Nick has a few mates out there. I'm sure he wouldn't mind giving you a bit of a tour of the camp fire scene.'

'No, not Nick,' Skye said with a trace of humour. 'Wynn would skin *me* alive, Jack.'

For a moment their gazes caught, and Skye's eyes widened as she read sudden determination in Jack's. He also said, 'I have plans for Wynn, Skye. Did you know there's a best-dress competition tonight? Well, there is, and I've just appointed famous model, Wynn Mortimer, as the judge. It should keep her out of mischief for at least an hour or so.' He stopped dancing and looked around.

'No. J-Jack, no...' Skye stammered.

But he took no notice of her and led her towards Nick, standing alone for a moment as someone danced off with Wynn.

Nick hesitated only briefly when told of Jack's mission. 'Why not?' he murmured. 'I've helped Skye with her books before. Let's go.'

'This wasn't my idea,' Skye said mutinously as he led her outside. 'So what you could do is walk me up to the house and I'll go to bed.'

'Not your idea to see what they're cooking on the camp fires?' He stopped walking and looked down at her enigmatically. He was in black tonight—shirt, trousers—although, like most of the men, he'd discarded his jacket and loosened his grey tie. It was a set of clothes Skye knew well and loved him in...

'Yes, of course that was my idea,' she said hastily. 'But...' She trailed off wearily.

'As in flying you out, I'd be the last person you'd ask to do this?' he supplied. 'Yet wasn't it you who suggested we could even be friends?'

'Nick,' she said tightly, '*you* seem to forget you're

here with another woman and my name is already dirt with her.'

He grinned. 'Don't worry about Wynn, Skye. All we're going to indulge in is an innocent little stroll around—aren't we?'

He looked so devastatingly alive and amused, she was torn between a desire to slap him or... No, she cautioned herself. Stop right there. She shrugged. 'All right.'

He found a friend, an opal prospector, who was more than happy to invite them to his camp fire. So they sat on a log, were introduced around, and handed tin plates. Nobody recognized Skye and seemed to have no idea that she and Nick had been engaged, so she found herself relaxing a little.

Someone twanged a guitar softly and she looked around the circle of people with interest. They were all prospectors with rough, dirt-engrained hands, or drovers, and people very used to camping out under the stars. Which was not to say they were roughing it food-wise, she discovered as she nibbled at a chicken wing and tried to analyse what it had been marinated in—it was delicious.

But the most interesting thing to her was how at ease Nick was with them and they with him. The firelight flickering on him couldn't have revealed someone from a different world more accurately than broad daylight, she mused. And not only because of the things it did reveal—his clothes and his clean, lean hands—but his aura.

Somehow or other you just knew that this was a clever man with a lot of clout—perhaps because of the way he spoke? Or perhaps because he could be so at ease amongst any company. Yet most of these people did seem to know him so he must have been prospecting with them and been down to their own grass-roots level.

Something he chose not to share with me, she thought sadly, and, with an effort, stopped looking at his hands...

'Wondered if you'd bring any of your fancy friends down to see us, Nick, me-old-cobber,' his friend Bluey said, but with no trace of offence in his voice.

'This particular friend,' Nick replied, 'was dying to see what you cook on your camp fires. She writes cookbooks.'

'Does she, now? What do you think of the chicken?' He turned to Skye.

'So much that I'd love to ask you for the recipe to put in my book. And...' Skye hesitated '...ask you if you have a recipe for witchety grubs, kangaroo-tail soup and...lizards?'

A shout of laughter went up round the camp fire. But again no one took offence and they started to regale Skye with the odd things they'd seen cooked and eaten, although it turned out that none of them had actually eaten witchety grubs or lizards. But they did come up with damper and bread recipes for her, and a few forms of bush tucker they had tried, which they obligingly wrote down on scraps of paper with much laughter as they agonized over their spelling.

But after the chicken bones had been removed and a potato in garlic butter baked in foil in the coals had been put on her plate with a spicy sausage and a portion of tomato and onion omelette she said that she might have to rethink her bush tucker chapter on Mount Gregory. Because the food was as tasty as if it had come from a gourmet kitchen.

They liked that. In fact it was soon obvious that they liked her a lot, and when they finally stood up to go Bluey drawled, 'If I were you, mate, I'd put a leg-rope on this little lady. 'Bout time you thought of getting hitched.'

Skye froze but Nick, with her hand in his, said lightly, 'Look who's calling the pot black. You've never been hitched to anyone in your life.'

'True, mate, true! But I only live one kind of life. You're never going to be able to be a real loner.'

'Is that what you want to be, Nick?'

They were wending their way back towards the marquee around another large, noisy tent—the boxing tent.

'Now that is an outback tradition,' he said. 'Know how it works?'

'No, but—'

'Members of the crowd are invited to take on one of the resident boxers who travel with the show. It can be quite funny.'

Skye shuddered. 'I hate boxing in any form.'

He didn't comment as they strolled past a beer-drinking contest.

'Aren't you going to answer, Nick?' she said at last. They were beside the race track now, a little away from all the activity, and he stopped and leant his elbows on the running rail.

There wasn't much grass on the Mount Gregory track; in fact the back straight was only sand, but this patch in front of the winning post was carefully nurtured and it looked cool and dewy in the starlight.

'Do I want to be a loner, Skye?' he said slowly. 'Not particularly but it could be the way I'm fashioned.'

She thought about this for a moment. 'When you're partying and driving racing cars et cetera, it doesn't look like it.'

'I once told you that's not all I like to do.'

She remembered the first time she'd had lunch with him. 'I know, but I never saw any evidence of it, or how you fitted in with this—' she gestured to take in the night and the place '—when we were—together.'

'I do it a lot less than I used to. But I've been coming up to this area since I was a kid, looking for opals, sapphires and gold. My father and I used to set off together in a truck with our swags and our billies and do just that. Then big business got in the way and he didn't have time to indulge his passion for what started it all for him.'

Skye was silent, trying to picture Nick as a little boy.

'Of course it's not only the joy of finding things,' he went on. 'It's the magic of the outback, the people, the wide open spaces, the folklore, things like this.' He gestured to include Mount Gregory.

She said a little helplessly, 'I said this before but when you're doing the other things you do it's hard to believe this side of you exists.'

He turned to look up at the stars and leant back

against the rail. 'Skye, what women may not under-stand about men and some of their preoccupations is this. Racing cars and boats is about speed, sure, but it's also a genuine fascination with motors and en-gines, how they tick and how to get the most out of them. The glamour and the social scene is only a by-product.'

'They do seem to go together,' she commented.

He shrugged. 'When you get as exhilarated as you do about technology and pushing limits, it seems to follow on naturally that you'd like to party.'

Skye looked at him with widening eyes. 'I never thought of it like that.'

He grimaced. 'Boxing is the same. Done properly, there's a science to it that appeals to a lot of men.'

'Well, I'm afraid you're not going to win me over there. And none of this—lesson on how to understand men explains why you feel you may be fashioned as a loner. Or why you didn't try to explain this better to me.'

'Perhaps it's because I couldn't explain it to my-self.'

Skye stared at him, wide-eyed.

'And perhaps,' he added, and moved his shoulders, 'Flo is right about me.'

'Your Florence?'

'The same,' he agreed. 'She reckons I've had too much handed to me on a platter and I'm too used to getting my own way. In other words, I don't take kindly to not being able to run the show.'

'Something I've never forgotten,' Skye mused as she digested this, 'is how secretly surprised your mother looked when she first met me. I don't know what's made me think of it now but...' She stopped and frowned.

'My mother *was* surprised because she read you more accurately than I did, and she also knows me well,' he said with a trace of grimness.

'Read me accurately as in how?' Skye queried.

He glanced down at her. 'Too much in love with me to know what you were getting yourself into, Skye.'

She gasped. 'But...but...look,' she stammered, then said desperately, 'How *does* one get fashioned as a loner? There must be reasons.'

'There's nothing deep or dark to do with my up-bringing, there's no unrequited love in my life that went badly wrong other than you, so—I guess Flo is right. I've led too much of a charmed life than is good for one, and it's my way of...sloughing it off.'

'I wouldn't have *clung*,' she whispered then stopped, appalled.

He put his arm around her and kissed the top of her head. 'You were always too good for me, Skye. Think of it that way. You were always meant to make someone a wonderful wife—'

'Don't you dare mention Bryce to me now,' she warned fiercely as tears came to her eyes.

'All right.'

'So it really is all over?' she said then, almost de-fiantly, as if to show she didn't care what he thought. 'If so, though, why did you do what you did to me last night?'

He smiled slightly. 'That was a very male ego talking.'

'But—'

'Skye, you were the one who saw it all more clearly than I did,' he said gently, and brushed the tears from her cheeks. 'By the way, I've been dying to ask you what you did with your wedding dress.'

She caught her breath because nothing could have killed any false hopes she'd been nurturing better than this query.

'Nothing,' she said huskily. 'It's still hanging up in, well, my mother's house. But I did cut the cake up into little pieces and I sent them all to a children's hospital.'

He smiled. 'I hope that made you feel better.'

'At the time it did. Nick…' She stopped.

'Go on,' he said quietly.

'You—only last night you said that I must have some regrets otherwise it didn't make sense. But you don't seem to have any at all.'

'If you're talking about Wynn—'

'Wynn herself has made it obvious there's more to you and her than there ever was between Bryce and me,' she pointed out.

'We're not sharing a room, Skye,' he said.

'That's because Sally told me she always gives everyone who is not married their own room on principle. Whatever happens from there on she has no control over.' She looked at him impatiently.

'So you've been imagining me creeping along the veranda in the dead of night?' He looked amused.

'It's not hard to imagine of Wynn,' Skye countered.

'Ah, but I do happen to respect Sally's principles,' he murmured.

Skye blinked. 'All the same—no regrets?'

'Of *course* there are regrets,' he said sombrely. 'But that doesn't change me, Skye.'

More tears rolled down her cheeks. 'I don't know if that makes me feel better or worse.'

He bent his head and kissed her lightly on the lips. 'If it's not Bryce, there's someone else out there for you. Funnily enough…' he paused thoughtfully '…it's how nice you are to him that makes me sure you're too good for me, Skye.'

'I *really* treat him like a younger brother, Nick,' she protested.

He shrugged. 'Perhaps that's it. You'd be good with kids, Skye. The way you got him to dance before—' he looked rueful '—he lost his footing was inspired. I'm good with machines and minerals, business, the stock market, but I don't somehow think I'd have much patience with kids.'

'All the same, Bryce is not a kid.'

He looked down at her with so much amusement now, she flinched visibly. Because he might as well have said that Bryce was light years behind him in worldliness and how to handle women.

Then he said quietly, 'If there's one thing I don't regret, Skye, it's…' He stopped as if unsure how to go on. 'Although I didn't altogether work you out accurately, I always knew there was something different about you, Skye. Now that I know what it is, I can only be glad I didn't change it.'

'I don't understand.' She frowned.

'Put it this way—months of sleeping with me could have—This is harder to say than I anticipated,' he murmured dryly.

'Do you mean that some of your worldliness and cynicism might have rubbed off?'

'Precisely.' He didn't look at all amused now. 'Then again, I don't know why I'm applauding myself for the fact that it didn't—'

'You were never worldly and cynical in bed, Nick,' she interrupted. 'Is it a problem now with Wynn?'

'Wynn knows how to play the game, Skye,' he said evenly.

'Does that mean she's also worldly and cynical?'

He didn't answer. Instead he turned her to face him and looked down at her with his lips twisted. 'I'm going to do something I shouldn't do now, Skye. Because I think we've said it all and I hope that this time I've done a better job of—accepting all the things you so accurately perceived as being wrong between us. Things that wouldn't have made for a happy marriage.'

She opened her mouth to speak but he touched her lips gently with his forefinger. 'Goodbye, Skye—to a relationship I should never have started with you. But I will always love you in a way and I'm sorry I was so unnecessarily brutal when we parted. Could we be friends? Perhaps we should give it a try.' And he bent his head to kiss her.

For an instant it was like old times. All the old sensations swept through her although his hands only rested on her lightly and his kiss was only brief. But the contact was enough to arouse an inner trembling and the lovely feeling of desire she was so afraid only Nick Hunter would be able to arouse in her.

And when it was finished she buried her face in his black shirt for an equally brief moment, but long enough to drink in the essence of this man through her senses and her pores—for the last time. Then she moved away and they started to walk towards the marquee.

'Skye?' he said gently.

'It's OK, Nick.' She tried to smile. 'I'm actually— I hated us parting in anger the way we did. So, now that I can't be angry with you any more, now that I don't feel it was all such a waste and that perhaps I *can* understand, I feel better. Friends?' She paused and grimaced. 'No, I don't think so. Let's just lay it to rest peacefully like this—for once and for all.'

CHAPTER FOUR

SHE dreamt that night of a cool, dewy patch of grass and a bunch of flowers lying on it in the starlight.

She woke up briefly to find that she'd been crying in her sleep, but when she woke the next morning she was curiously calm. It crossed her mind that she might have at last laid her relationship with Nick to rest.

However, there was still another day to get through, not to mention some speculation to endure about what had happened to her the night before. She'd asked Nick to take her up to the house and he'd complied although he'd gone back to the ball himself. Perhaps he'd explained that she was simply tired out? She devoutly hoped so.

One bright spark to this new day, she discovered when she got to a rather subdued breakfast gathering, was that Maggie had joined the house party. Another—she found herself breathing a sigh of relief—was the non-appearance of Wynn. So that apart from a couple of curious glances from Bryce there was not so much to endure at all.

Just Nick, she thought, just Nick... And waited for the familiar pain to close around her heart as he sat down at the table on the veranda in the same clothes he'd worn two days ago when she'd arrived.

It didn't happen and she was able to turn her attention to Mary and her grandmother's cookbook gratefully. If she wasn't cured, she was certainly anaesthetized.

Although, even anaesthetized in the region of her heart, her antennae were still unusually sensitive, she discovered. Because, while she could genuinely enthuse over the old leather-bound volume stuffed with handwritten recipes—some calling for a dozen eggs!—and the delightful drawings in the margins, she could still tune into Nick's conversation with Bryce and Maggie.

And it dawned on her that Nick was skilfully and subtly doing what she herself had hoped to do. Which was to draw Bryce and Maggie together via their similar interests and their recent accidents. Maggie was ruefully explaining that it had been her own clumsiness that had seen her fall off the boat and break her arm when she hit the duckboard. Which was strange, she'd gone on to add, because she was really at home *in* the water...

Why was Nick doing it? Skye wondered, somewhat stunned, as Bryce began to confide his own difficulties out of the water. Had he decided Bryce wasn't the one for her? But what did it matter to him now, anyway?

The table was cleared while all this was going on and deliciously fragrant coffee served. Then Wynn trod out onto the veranda with the utmost delicacy. She wore white jeans, a scarlet blouse tied in a knot at her midriff and a large pair of dark glasses.

'Don't talk to me, anybody, please,' she said

faintly. 'I have a killer hangover and I'm liable to bite. If I could just have some black, strong coffee...'

Mary sat up immediately and paged through her book. 'There's a wonderful cure for hangovers in here. Let me see—raw eggs and—'

But Jack intervened as Wynn looked sickened. 'Try this.' He put a glass of tomato juice down in front of her.

'Not a Bloody Mary—Jack, you wouldn't be so *civilized* as to have made me a fair dinkum—'

'I would,' Jack said shortly. 'But you weren't particularly civilized yourself last night.'

'Then you shouldn't have been so free with the champagne, Jack, dear,' Wynn responded with a definite bite in her voice. 'In fact I'm forced to wonder whether you connived to get me drunk so Skye here—dear, silly Skye—could lure Nick away to try for a reunion! If you felt like that—' she turned to Skye and went on with pure venom '—you should never have let him go in the first place.'

Nick stood up, pulled Wynn to her feet and propelled her indoors.

'What...happened?' Skye heard herself asking cautiously.

It was Bryce who explained while everyone else looked immeasurably embarrassed. 'She accosted Nick in the middle of the floor and tried to pour a bottle of champagne over him. He caught her hand just in time so most of it went over her—'

He broke off to look briefly amused. 'She then started to berate him in very unladylike language, during the course of which she made several references along the lines of—what had he thought he was doing, anyway, to bring her to this Hicksville neck of the woods, and surrounding her with the most ultimate hicks she'd ever met in her life? All of which,' Bryce concluded, 'was audible to everyone in the tent.'

'That was rather masterly, Bryce,' Jack remarked. 'I've never seen such a disgraceful exhibition in my life. Heaven *alone* knows why Nick—'

'Because he was looking for the exact opposite of Skye, Jack,' Sally said impatiently. 'Why are men so blind? And to be honest, before Skye arrived—sorry, Skye—but all the same we found ourselves quite liking Wynn.'

'I knew I should never have stayed.' Skye stood up. 'I'm so sorry—'

'Sit down, Skye,' Nick said authoritatively, coming out through the French doors. 'Look, my apologies to everyone—and Wynn is now feeling very sick and sorry for herself but she's prepared to apologize too. She has asked for your understanding—she's been under a lot of pressure lately. But if you'd rather we left, Jack and Sally, I'd quite understand.'

It was Sally who said slowly, 'I think Skye is the one who deserves an apology.'

'Undoubtedly, but what you may not realize is that Skye has a lot more inner fortitude than Wynn, who is not that confident under her glossy exterior.'

Everyone did a double take.

'Well,' Jack said slowly, 'well, in that case—'

'Don't go, Nick,' Sally finished for him.

'Are you quite sure, Sal?'

Sally and Jack nodded together.

'Then—' Nick picked up a cup of coffee and the Bloody Mary, '—I'll see if these help her—'

'Water,' Skye heard herself say. 'She should drink a lot of water.'

He dipped his head in her direction and went inside again.

'You're very sweet, my dear,' Mary said admiringly.

'I'm not really.' Skye shrugged. 'I've said a few unkind things to her but I didn't know...' She stopped and frowned. It was Bryce who put into words the thoughts that were running through her mind.

'I wonder if he's only being a friend to her?'

'I don't think she quite sees it that way, but, you never know,' Jack contributed.

Sally stood up in a way that was rather obviously meant to quash any further discussion on the subject of Nick and Wynn, and said brightly, 'It's the same timetable today, early lunch then down to the track, but could you come to lunch already dressed for the races? It's a bigger program today so it starts earlier. Skye, Jack and I would like you to present the Mount Gregory Cup for the feature race today so would you like to come and choose another hat?'

'Well, I'm going to wear my grey dress—the one I wore the first night—so—Why didn't he just take her home?' Skye turned from Sally's hats to look at their owner. 'Unlike me, he doesn't have to rely on lifts or anything.'

'I don't know. I wish he had but we've known Nick

a long time—I can't work out why he never brought you up here, Skye!'

'Neither can I, but that was one of our problems. We lived in a bubble, just the two of us, for the most part—How about this one?' She turned away to pick out a hat.

Sally looked at her back wisely and said only. 'It might have been made for your dress, Skye.'

Skye turned back and twirled the white hat on her hand. It was small and very chic. A pillbox with a taffeta bow on the top and a pert, concealing little veil. 'You have wonderful taste in hats, Sally. Thanks!' She hugged the other woman quickly then went away to her room.

And on this morning she did what she'd said she was going to do yesterday. She opened her laptop and worked away doggedly on her book until it was time to get ready.

Wynn was at lunch looking subdued and dressed almost conservatively in a beige linen dress and a simple straw hat. She waited until everyone was seated then quietly and sincerely apologized for her awful behaviour, especially towards Skye.

There was an awkward little silence then Skye raised her glass and said, 'Wynn, I just hope that when I have to make a public apology—and I guess it can happen to all of us—I can do it as well as that. Here's to you.'

Everyone took up the toast and soon things at Mount Gregory homestead were back to normal.

*　　*　　*

'I didn't know you were part of the presentation,' Skye said to Nick as he led her out to the patch of lawn in front of the winning post.

He looked her up and down, at the taffeta flower on top of her hat, her eyes behind the mesh of her veil, her severely pinned-up hair, her grey dress with which she wore a short white bolero with cap sleeves and a stand-up collar, and the tips of her stockinged toes in her silver sandals. 'Or you mightn't have agreed to it?' he suggested.

'Well, no, I might not have,' she said slowly, taking in his beautiful lightweight grey suit worn with a darker grey shirt and a charcoal tie.

'Why?'

She stopped and sighed. They'd come to a table on which the Mount Gregory Cup sat in all its glory with two smaller cups beside it. There was a microphone and there was a crowd gathered on the other side of the running rail. One tired horse was being led around and its connections were starting to gather. And suddenly her nerves started to tighten.

'I don't know why I agreed to it at *all*,' she looked around anxiously '—but thank heavens you're—I mean, what are you doing here, Nick? I don't have to make any speeches, do I?' she added tautly.

'I'm the MC today, a man of many talents,' he said wryly. 'And all you have to do is look beautiful and hand over the cups. Looking beautiful is not a problem, by the way.'

'Oh. Thanks.' She coloured suddenly under his scrutiny.

'I see you've improvised again.' He touched one

front corner of the white grosgrain bolero. It ended just below her breasts and didn't meet at the centre but it nevertheless provided a touch of afternoon chic to a dress she normally wore in the evenings.

She shrugged and said a little helplessly, 'That's how you do it. Shawls, boleros and so on. I mean change an outfit. Nick—'

'You were also very gracious towards Wynn, Skye,' he added quietly as he raised the microphone to his height. 'Thank you.'

Skye opened her mouth impulsively to say, Does she mean so much to you? But fortunately he started to speak into the mike and the moment was lost.

There was a roar from the crowd when he introduced her and the owners, trainer and jockey of the winning horse looked immensely gratified to receive their trophies from the hands of Skye Belmont. Then it was all over and she heaved a sigh of relief and started to walk back along the track towards the tent.

'By the way, were you doing what I thought you were doing before all the drama at breakfast this morning?' she asked curiously, feeling almost light-headed with relief.

He stopped in the middle of the track and looked down at her with a raised eyebrow.

'Trying to bring Bryce and Maggie together,' she enunciated a little impatiently.

'Yes, as a matter of fact, I was.'

'Why?'

'Don't tell me it didn't occur to you that they might have an awful lot in common, Skye?'

She shrugged. 'Yes, it did. And I was going to, well—'

'Do a little matchmaking of your own?' he supplied with a wicked glint.

'Yes. But I have a vested interest. You don't,' she pointed out. 'In fact, ever since I arrived you've done your best to push me towards him.'

'I've changed my mind. A budding marine biologist who also has trouble coping with dry land—well, a boat, but nevertheless who happens to be living in Townsville, which is not that far from Cairns, has to be pretty nearly perfect for Bryce Denver.'

'I do know all that—'

'Besides which,' Nick went on serenely, 'I know you have his best interests at heart.'

Skye made a little sound like a frustrated kitten but he led her towards a gate in the running rail and what she was about to say was lost as she passed through and an excited crowd raced up to engulf her.

It was terrifying; she'd not been expecting it, neither had Nick, and it took him a few moments to control things and give her a bit of breathing space.

'That was my fault, sorry,' he said grimly. 'OK? I think if you sign a few race books they'll be happy.'

Skye swallowed. 'All right.' So she did for a little while, even managing to laugh and chat with the crowd, but anyone looking at her closely would have noticed that she was taking very deep breaths.

Then someone called out, 'Are you two back together? You must have been mad to let her go, Nicky, boy!'

Skye froze but Nick said easily at large, 'Don't I

know it? Thanks, everyone—here come the horses for the next race.'

The crowd melted away and he took her hand and led her away.

'Where are we going?' she asked with difficulty.

'Out of sight,' he said with that trace of grimness back in his voice.

The out-of-sight he provided for them was two folding chairs behind Jack's Land Rover, which was parked well away from the proceedings, and he procured two glasses of champagne on the way.

'Thanks.' Skye sank down and sipped her champagne.

'Are you all right? You went so pale—you still are. What a fool I was,' he said roughly.

'I got a fright; I just wasn't expecting it, that's all,' she said ruefully. 'Well…' She stopped and grimaced.

'It must have happened to you before.'

'Only once… The thing is,' she said sadly, 'while I know they only mean well, I suffer from an awful form of claustrophobia when that happens. I'm not morbid about it, I just…get a bit breathless.'

He frowned. 'You never told me this. And you did go walkabout on your own yesterday. You didn't have to agree to do this today, either.'

'I was pretty heavily disguised yesterday, remember? That's how I go to the supermarket these days. And today—I don't know why I agreed,' she said helplessly. 'So much has happened, I guess, I wasn't thinking straight. But I honestly didn't think many people out here would know who Skye Belmont was. Your friends last night didn't.'

'Why didn't you ever tell me, though?' he demanded.

'I'm not proud of it.' She shrugged.

'But the station knows, obviously?'

'Yes,' she agreed. 'But they had to. I…well, I nearly fainted the first time it happened. So now any appearances I do are very carefully controlled. I can't believe I'm such a wimp!' she said with genuine exasperation.

'We've been out together, Skye,' he said slowly, 'and you've never worn a disguise.'

'Only to places where they're not in the habit of mobbing people, Nick. And the few times I did come to the race track with you or that kind of place, *you* may not have thought I was disguised but I did take the trouble not to be instantly recognizable, or wander off. Besides…' She paused on the point of saying that she'd always felt safe with him, then thought better of it.

He looked at her with frustration written clear in his eyes. 'I still can't understand why you didn't tell me.'

'Perhaps I didn't think it fitted in with the Skye Belmont you thought I was,' she said barely audibly.

Slow comprehension dawned in his eyes. 'You genuinely believe this is a wimpish kind of weakness, don't you?'

She shrugged. 'I certainly wish I could rid myself of it.'

'In fact, you're exceptionally brave, Skye,' he said gently.

'Oh, no, Nick—'

'No one would have known and now you've done it once you may find you can do it again.'

'I only managed to do it because you were—' She stopped abruptly. 'I mean I'm quite sure Bryce could have taken care of me, or Jack—'

'Bryce?' His scepticism was obvious.

She licked her lips. 'Fully functional, of course.'

'I wonder?' he said coolly.

'Anyway, it's not your problem,' she tried to say gaily. 'Don't you think we should join the others? Look, Nick,' she went on when he made no move, 'it's not that serious. I wouldn't be able to go around with any confidence, even disguised if it were. Do I look a traumatized kind of person? I'm not; it's just one small thing that's a problem, that's all.'

'Don't you feel safe with anyone else?'

'Of course! Six husky security guards make the world of difference!'

'Skye, don't joke about it.'

'But don't you see? It's because I can that I know it's not that serious.'

His eyes told her that he didn't believe a word of it. 'I should have guessed,' he murmured as if to himself. 'The wig, the big hat yesterday, the veil today—the way, now I think of it, you never wear your hair in public as you do on your program.' He paused. 'And, of course, the night before when you were talking about being dysfunctional—it was to do with this, wasn't it?'

She shrugged. But his gaze was dark and compelling as he stared at her. And, although she would have given anything to be able to resist it, it was as if he was mentally drawing her into his arms and surrounding her with his strength and protection. It was as if he were making love to her with his mind…

It had, she found to her horror, the most devastating effect on her. It made her think of all the times she'd lain in his arms delirious with delight, because he made her body sing to a tune like no other.

It brought back to mind how, when they were still together, he would, with one look, indicate to her that he intended to extricate them to some private place where he'd be at liberty to undress her and stroke her breasts, tease her nipples with his teeth and run his fingers along the pale, silky skin of her inner thighs before inflicting such pleasure on her…

'Nick, don't,' she whispered hoarsely, and stood up abruptly.

'Two minds thinking alike, I believe,' he said sombrely, and stood up too. 'Skye—'

'No,' she gasped. 'You're the one who can't or won't change! You're the one who told me only last night that it really was over—don't think you can still do this to me, Nick. I'm not some mindless slave to sex; there has to be more to it.'

'It wasn't just sex,' he said harshly. 'Do you really see it like that?'

'It wasn't much more.'

'Well, I tell you what, Skye. Come back to me when you've had a chance to experiment with other men. Then we might be able to compare notes. And resolve exactly what it may have been.'

Her lips parted and her eyes widened in sheer shock. 'Nick,' she said unsteadily but intensely, 'do you honestly think I'd have been able to hide something like this—' she waved a hand in the direction of where she'd been mobbed '—from you if we'd been true soul mates?' And she turned and fled from him.

Nick Hunter watched her disappear into the tent, and ground his teeth in extreme frustration as he asked himself why the hell he couldn't just let Skye Belmont go. She had a point, of course, although she had obviously gone out of her way to hide it. But… The thing is, he mused savagely, there was no way he could transform himself into the kind of husband she wanted and, to make matters worse, he now had a sudden insight into why she needed a husband who was always there. Did she understand, could she ever understand it was her claustrophobia that magnified his problem with being tied down, though?

So why, he asked himself, did he feel as if he'd let her down?

Dinner was a low-key meal that night, a buffet, and to Skye's relief no one suggested dancing afterwards.

Sally brought out some cards and the men, and Wynn, started to play poker while the other women sat around and chatted.

Wynn was back on top form, having left the races early, apparently, to have a rest. And she was proving herself to be a daring poker player.

Then Bryce got a call from his pilot friend to say that he was stranded in Weipa with a malfunctioning nose wheel and it would be a couple of days at least before he could get back to Mount Gregory to pick Bryce and Skye up.

'Damn!' Bryce put the satellite phone down. 'I'm due back at work the day after tomorrow.'

'Well, I don't think I'll be airborne by then but I'm sure I can work something out for you, mate,' Jack said, and turned to Nick as if struck by inspiration. 'You could fit two more in, couldn't you? Especially as Skye travels so light,' he added humorously.

Jack! Skye said to herself internally. Look what happened the last time you brought Nick and me together!

But Nick merely said easily, 'Sure. No problems. So long as they don't mind an early start tomorrow.' And Wynn didn't miss a beat.

Bryce breathed a sigh of relief then looked troubled as he glanced at Skye.

She immediately said, 'I've got a ticket to Sydney so as long as I can get back to Cairns I'll be fine. I may even spend a day or two there.'

She wasn't sure, as she stopped speaking, whether anyone else spotted the brief, sardonic look Nick cast her over his shoulder. But she ignored it and turned back to the recipes she was copying out of Mary's grandmother's cookbook.

And presently she took herself to bed.

The next morning she hugged Jack and Sally and thanked them warmly. She also assured Mary and Sally she would send them a signed copy of her cookbook, and noted out of the corner of her eye that Bryce and Maggie were exchanging phone numbers.

Then they were taxiing down the runway in Nick's comfortable six-seater plane. The flight passed in a bit of a blur for Skye, though. She didn't want to watch how relaxed yet professional Nick was as a pilot, she certainly didn't want to see much of Wynn and, although she was fairly sure Bryce was interested in Maggie despite himself, she knew she would have to handle a parting of their ways with care.

They landed in a muggy, overcast Cairns and Nick made no attempt to persuade her to fly on to Sydney with them. They said goodbye casually and no one would have known they'd been lovers, let alone friends. Wynn was also friendly but casual.

Even Bryce, as he ushered her towards his car in the security car park, seemed unusually quiet.

She told him that she'd spend at least one night in a hotel, so he suggested the Hilton and drove her into town. On the way, she nerved herself to say what she had to but he suddenly forestalled her.

'Would it be all right, Skye, if we were friends?'

'Well—'

'I know what you're going to say—there's no point and I'll get hurt, but I think I'm over that.'

Skye glanced at him.

'For two reasons,' he continued. 'I know I could never make you feel the way Nick does and, while I think I'll always love you in a way, I may have found someone—more attainable.'

Skye was struck silent for a good minute. Then she said with a kind of dread, 'Don't tell me it shows that much.'

'With Nick? No. But I knew what to look for.'

'The whole world knew about us, Bryce—'

'But they don't know the real Skye Belmont. They didn't spend time with her on Haggerstone Island, they didn't see her at Mount Gregory as I did.'

'And that tells you something about me, Bryce?' she said slowly.

'That you're the kind of girl who only gives herself to one man, Skye.'

She sighed and looked at her clasped hands resting in her lap. 'I hope not, Bryce, but yes, you're right; it's going to take me a long time to get over Nick. By the way—' she turned to him impulsively '—didn't I tell you there was someone out there for you? Maggie is lovely.'

'There's nothing between us yet,' he began.

'No, but go for it. And thanks; I will always love you in a way too.'

He pulled up in front of the Hilton. 'Will you be all right? Unfortunately I'm working on a research ship at the moment, and we're heading out to the reef tomorrow morning for a week—'

'I'll be fine. Look—' she pulled a card from her purse '—write to me and tell me how it's going. I promise I'll write back. And thanks again for everything!' She leant towards him and kissed him lightly.

She spent the rest of the day in her room, writing. She also decided she would spend a couple of days in Cairns; at least it put off going home and she liked Cairns anyway. It was colourfully tropical and laid-back. More a big town than a small city, it was situated on the Trinity Inlet and was home to a fishing fleet as well as all sorts of dive and cruise boats that went out to the Great Barrier Reef, and there were some very nice restaurants.

It was thinking of these that made her arch her back and rub her neck, then close down her laptop and decide to go out for a meal.

She put on a striped T-shirt, baggy denim dungarees, her boots and a baseball cap pulled down low with her hair crammed up into it. Looking at herself from under its peak, she hesitated then put on a pair of lightly tinted John Lennon glasses. That would do it, she decided, and, picking up a backpack-style bag, she slung it over her shoulder and went to see Cairns.

The first person she bumped into in the foyer was Nick. Literally bumped into as she stepped out of the lift and he turned from talking to a bellhop to step into it.

'What are you...?' She gasped, giving herself away immediately as she tried to regain her balance.

'Skye.' He held onto her until she was steady on her feet again, and looked down at her with his lips twisting. 'Fairly effective,' he drawled, 'although I think I still would have known you before you opened your mouth.'

'What are you doing here, though?' she said tautly. 'You should be in Sydney!'

'If you'll allow me, I'll explain.' He drew her into the lift, pressed a button and they began to ascend.

'But...where...? Look,' she said disjointedly, 'I don't want to go anywhere with you, let alone your room!'

'Anyone would think you're a shy virgin, Skye.

What do you think I might do to you? Make love to you against your will?' He raised a mocking eyebrow at her.

She coloured visibly even beneath the peak of her cap.

'All I want to do is wait for my luggage to come up then we could go out and do whatever you like,' he added. 'I take it you've disguised yourself again so you could go out for a meal?' This time there was amusement as well as mockery in his expression.

'Yes,' she said stonily. 'And you don't have to make it sound so...silly!'

'My apologies,' he murmured. 'Here we are.'

Skye hesitated, then, because her room was on the same floor and because she'd suddenly lost all enthusiasm for eating out in Cairns, she stepped out of the lift.

But when he stopped in front of a door she said, 'I don't believe this! Did you ask for this room?'

'No. Why?'

Her gaze travelled involuntarily to the next door.

He followed it. 'I see—you wouldn't be right next door by any chance, Skye?'

'Yes,' she said through her teeth. 'Did you know I was in this hotel?' she asked ominously.

'Well, I always stay at the Hilton but as a matter of fact I did.' He glanced over his shoulder as a door opened on the other side and two people came out. At the same time the lift opened and more people arrived on the floor.

He turned back to her. 'Going to come in quietly, Skye, or would you like me to come to your room?

It doesn't matter to me but one or the other I intend to do, even if it takes a scene.'

'You wouldn't,' she breathed.

But he assured her quietly that he would and when he unlocked his door she followed him in.

'That was despicable!' she stormed, taking her cap off and tossing it onto the bed.

He smiled slightly. As he had been all day, he was wearing khaki trousers, a khaki cotton battle jacket and a plain white shirt. 'I don't think I've ever seen you in a rage before, Skye. Like a drink?'

'No, thank you!'

'Well, I'm going to have a beer. I've been flying people around the country all day.'

He opened the mini-bar and withdrew not only a beer but a half-bottle of white wine.

She watched him incredulously as he opened it, poured a glass and brought it over to her. He said, 'Don't be childish, Skye.' And removed her spectacles.

She glared at him, compressed her lips then took the glass ungraciously.

'Excuse me,' he murmured, at a knock on the door, and went to deal with his luggage.

Skye walked over to the window and studied Cairns through it. The day had cleared up and there was a fine sunset gilding the Inlet and Cape Grafton across it. It wouldn't take long for dark to fall, as was the way in the tropics. But beyond these observations crossing her mind she found herself desperately searching for an explanation for *this*. None came.

When they were alone again, she turned to face the

room, to say with a sudden defeated movement of her shoulders, 'I don't understand. How did you know I was here anyway?'

'I got in touch with Bryce.'

'*Bryce!* How?'

'Through Jack. Sit down, Skye.'

'I'll stand, thank you.'

He shrugged and sank down into an armchair, running his fingers idly through his dark hair. He said with a glimmer of amusement, 'Are you surprised that Bryce divulged your whereabouts?'

'I…no. Uh…I mean…' She couldn't go on.

'You mean you've sorted things out with him?'

'I mean——he sorted things out for himself,' she said gloomily, then immediately looked wary. 'He decided he would always love me in a way but Maggie was more attainable; that's what I meant.'

'And you're feeling a little let down?' Nick suggested.

'Not at all,' she protested, and sat down opposite him without stopping to think. 'What do you think I am? Well,' she conceded with a sudden little glint of humour of her own, 'men are strange sometimes, I guess, but I can only thank heavens Maggie came along.'

'That's it?'

'We're going to write and be friends,' she said—unwisely, as it happened. 'But he probably won't even do that.'

Nick drank some beer. 'I think it would be a good idea if you extended a hand of friendship to me, Skye, talking of this. That's why I'm here, incidentally.'

Her glass tilted and she spilt some drops of wine on her dungarees. 'What do you mean?' she asked incredulously as she dabbed at the spots with her fingertip. 'Look, we've been through it all, said all there is to say—'

'No, we haven't—'

'And been through more than was necessary when you come to think of it,' she went on heedlessly, as memories of the night he'd reminded her of their nude swim swept over her.

'But we haven't really been over this and I'm worried about you. More so than ever.' He looked meaningfully over to the bed where her cap and glasses lay.

She sighed and sat back. 'Oh, that—I wish I'd never told you.'

'Does your mother know?'

'Yes. Nick, perhaps this is what we should be discussing if we're going to discuss anything—what have you done with Wynn?'

He paused and looked at her thoughtfully. 'What has that got to do with it?'

'I'm not entirely reassured she will be all sweetness and light towards me and you being friends or even doing this together,' Skye murmured with some irony.

'Don't worry, she's not liable to appear on the scene and try to empty a champagne bottle all over me,' he said with a wicked little grin.

Skye grimaced. 'You were the one who told me she knew how to play the game—whatever that means. A relationship with no strings, no clinging? If so, I'm wondering whether you were quite wrong.'

He sat forward. 'Yes, I was wrong. That's why Wynn is on Hamilton Island, a couple of days early for a modelling assignment. I flew her there instead of Sydney.'

'So…what…how—I don't understand,' Skye said a little helplessly.

He shrugged and looked at his beer meditatively. 'Wynn is a friend of my sister. She and Pippa went to school together all their lives so I've known her for years and years. When I bumped into her after we broke up, she was in a similar situation—she'd been ditched in other words,' he said dryly.

'I didn't ditch you,' Skye protested.

'No? It felt like it, strange to say; anyway—'

'Look here, Nick,' Skye broke in determinedly, 'was Wynn passed over for another woman?'

He stared at her. 'Yes, but—'

'Then that is being ditched as I understand it. And it's not what I did to you.'

'Forgive me—' he inclined his head towards her '—I'll have to watch my semantics, but, whatever—when I suddenly found myself sans you, Skye, and not being in a very pleasant frame of mind, it seemed like a good idea for Wynn and I, seeing how long we'd known each other, to—console each other.'

'I can imagine,' Skye said darkly.

'I'm not sure that you can—'

Skye waved a hand. 'Don't. I don't want to hear and I don't care.'

He paused, then said, 'You did bring Wynn up.'

'All right. And you're trying to tell me she became not only possessive but *clinging* even, which is why she's now cooling her heels on Hamilton Island—sans you, Nick? Well, I've got the picture; I just don't see what it's got to do with me.'

He got up and poured some more wine into her glass and paced around the room before stopping in front of her. 'We're going to fight this fear of crowds, you and I, Skye, and we need to be friends to do it. That's all.'

CHAPTER FIVE

'You must be mad, Nick,' Skye said huskily, when she could speak.

He simply shrugged. 'Finish your wine and we'll go out to dinner.'

'I've lost all desire to go out to dinner!'

He grinned. 'You may think you have but I'm seriously starving—by the way, I only have dinner in mind. I wouldn't dream of trying to—make you a slave to sex afterwards.'

Her eyes darkened. 'That's just as well because you wouldn't succeed.'

'They were your words, Skye,' he pointed out. 'However...' he paused and something cool and determined glinted in his eyes '...I'm quite capable of keeping you here until you agree.'

She gasped. 'You wouldn't!'

'Yes, I would,' he drawled, 'so take your pick—dinner here in the room with me or dinner out.'

Skye drained her glass and put it down with a snap as she stood up. 'Just this once, Nick. I had no idea you could be such a bully!'

He looked amused but as she reached for her baseball cap and glasses it faded and he said quietly, 'No, Skye.'

'But I...'

He took them from her and put them back on the bed. 'Just brush your hair,' he advised.

She fought a tense little battle with herself and not only to do with going out in public undisguised. There was also a foolish element to do with trying to prove a point to Nick, only she wasn't quite sure what the point was.

Whatever it was, it won, and she fumbled in her bag for a brush, muttering beneath her breath, and started to brush out her hair.

He waited patiently with his hands shoved into the pockets of his khaki trousers, and because she could see him in the dressing-table mirror Skye discovered she had something else to contend with on top of the sheer shock of this turn of events—an acute sense of *déjà vu*.

They'd often laughed at the battles she had with her hair, and her expressed wish for straight, smooth locks that did what they were told...

How many times had she brushed her hair in front of a mirror with him watching her? How often had she done it with no clothes on because she'd slipped out of bed with the first thing on her mind being the taming of her riotous curls? Only to find herself being returned to bed because, as he'd put it, there was something irresistible about her naked in front of a mirror with her arms raised and a serious expression on her face, not to mention the perfection of her hips.

She put the brush down abruptly then shoved it into her bag, along with her cap and glasses, and said briefly, 'Let's go.'

He didn't move for a long moment but she refused to look at him, and they left in silence.

Skye sat back and patted her stomach with a contented sigh.

She'd just eaten the most delicious garlic prawns on a bed of rice with an Italian salad. They were in a restaurant on a boardwalk overlooking the Inlet; it was bright and noisy and the view of the boats in the marina and skimming along the dark water was fascinating.

'I take it you approve of the food here, Miss Belmont?' Nick said.

'I do,' Skye agreed, and rinsed her fingers. Slices of lemon and little white flowers floated in the finger bowl. She dried her hands on a large white linen napkin. 'Not only that but the way they do things—no paper serviettes, for example.'

'Nor has it been too difficult being here as yourself?'

She thought for a bit as she watched the view. She had been recognized and a few people had come to ask for her autograph. The chef had also come out to meet her and the proprietor had asked if he could take a photo to put on the wall. But Nick had been recognized as well and it was not hard to feel the flow of interest directed at their table. Something had given her the serenity to cope with it all, though.

That strange desire to prove a mysterious point to him? she asked herself. It had to be more than that, though, considering her state of mind when she'd left the hotel with him.

'Skye?'

She looked back at him and wished acutely that he were not so devastatingly attractive as he leant his elbows on the table and watched her. Not only physically but there was no denying he could be incredibly nice when he put his mind to it. As he had been ever since they'd sat down. There'd been no sign, she thought ruefully, of the man who had virtually hijacked her. It could probably be truthfully said that he'd charmed her right out of her sulks.

'Nick, two things,' she murmured. 'This is not a real test because you—well, you seem to have the authority to—make people behave reasonably. Somehow—' she tipped a hand '—when you indicate that enough is enough they take notice. And secondly there's going to be an awful lot of speculation about us now.'

'Let them speculate,' he said idly. 'I've always found "no comment" is the best way to deal with it, incidentally.'

'OK. But there's another thing.' She hesitated briefly and frowned. 'I don't think it's so unnatural to want to dodge public attention at times—do you?'

'Not at all.' He sat back. 'I do it frequently. When ᵼt comes to *all* the time, it could be different. In other woᵣds, it could be starting to be a phobia.'

She wrinkled her brow again. 'I've never liked crowds so it may not have anything to do with being slightly famous.'

One dark eyebrow shot up. 'Slightly?'

'Well,' she said, and paused. 'Why *are* cooks so...so...?'

'Powerfully interesting to the public?' he suggested. 'I guess because eating is one of the main pleasures of life. In your case, it's also your personality and the fact that you're very lovely, but, as two fat ladies could tell you, that's not necessarily a prerequisite.'

She smiled. 'I love them!'

'They'd probably love you. Feeling faint and dizzy, breathless and nauseous, though, Skye, is not natural,' he said quietly.

'So what do you suggest I do?' she asked perplexedly, for two reasons. She didn't remember telling him all the symptoms she suffered. And she couldn't imagine what he was going to suggest. 'It's no good going out and fainting, Nick; even you must see that.'

'No. But there could be a hidden reason for it, something that you may well be able to conquer. Phobias are not unknown for having their roots in very strange places.' His dark eyes were suddenly compelling.

'You sound like your mother,' Skye said, and stopped abruptly. 'Have you...?'

'Yes, I spoke to my mother about it. Also your mother, Skye—'

'When?' She stared at him incredulously.

'Today.'

'You've been very busy on the phone today,' she said bitterly. 'Look, I wish you hadn't worried my mother; she's worried enough about me as it is—' She broke off, annoyed.

'Because of me?' he queried.

'Because of me,' she contradicted him.

'In the context of me, then?' The expression in his dark eyes was satirical.

Skye clicked her tongue exasperatedly. 'It doesn't matter.'

'Well, it so happens that she wasn't worried about you in a claustrophobic context because she didn't know.' He watched her with some irony.

Skye opened her mouth but nothing came out.

'Oh,' he said, 'she knew that you sometimes wore a wig et cetera—'

'Nick,' Skye said wearily, 'all right, I didn't ever tell her that much about it. I'm an only child and now my father is dead she has nothing else to worry about.'

'OK, point taken.' He played with the salt-cellar for a moment. 'But when, on my mother's advice, I suggested to *your* mother that this just might go back to something in your childhood, and may never have surfaced the way it has if you hadn't become famous, she agreed that indeed it could.'

'How, what and *why*?'

He looked at her meditatively. 'I think we might be better off going into that somewhere less public.'

Skye was too unwillingly fascinated to resist.

They found a dark corner of a bar in the Radisson Hotel, and ordered coffee and liqueurs.

'Do you remember getting lost in a shopping centre when you were five?' he asked as they sat next to each other on a curved banquette.

Skye shook her head.

'It was close to Christmas, your mother says. It was

extremely crowded. She turned away briefly and when she turned back you'd disappeared. It was twenty minutes before she found you and, to increase her panic-stricken state, you seemed to have gone into a trance. She couldn't get you to talk—for about an hour afterwards.'

Skye stared at him, her eyes widening.

'You were wearing a yellow dress,' he said slowly, 'with white sandals and a yellow ribbon in your hair. You had your own little purse, a plastic one with white daisies on a yellow background, and you were going to look for a Christmas present for your father. You couldn't make up your mind whether you'd like to buy a tie or a book about golf. He was golf-mad, your father, according to your mother.'

He paused as Skye stared into the distance, blinking rapidly.

'But before you got a chance to buy anything she lost you, and she finally found you wedged into a corner between a red mail box and a phone booth—'

'Orange and blue,' Skye said, and started to breathe erratically.

He put an arm around her and held her close until her breathing subsided.

'Why didn't I remember it?' she whispered, her eyes still big and agitated.

'As you said, you were an only child.' He still spoke slowly and quietly. 'A very precious little person who was never wittingly exposed to any danger, and you hadn't even started school. That's why you got such a fright. All those people milling around, tripping over you, perhaps, carrying you along, away from your mother.' He stopped and stroked her hair as she shuddered.

'That's what the doctor said when your parents consulted him, although, by then, you seemed to be completely back to normal. What worried them all was that you didn't even seem to remember it.'

'I must have blocked it out! How—bizarre!'

'Indeed, but not all that uncommon. Anyway, they watched you for years but all they could detect was a slight aversion to crowds.' He shrugged. 'A lot of people don't like crowds. Your mother herself doesn't.'

Skye closed her eyes and shuddered again. 'I tried to open the door of the phone booth but I couldn't, then I didn't want to in case I got stuck inside. Why haven't they triggered this memory—mail boxes and—? Hang on,' she said huskily. 'I will do almost anything in my power to avoid having to make a call from a phone booth because of a nameless kind of dread I have of them.'

He said nothing and she rested against him as her memory fled back down the years and presented her, with astonishing clarity, with something she'd been too frightened to ever think of again. The sandals she wore with a sundress and matching ribbons in her hair, the awful sensation of being absolutely alone amidst so many people, the cool painted metal of the mail box as she'd clung to it…

They must have sat like that for a good ten minutes while she haltingly talked about it, telling him every-thing. And gradually, as she talked, her remembered panic began to subside and she could think of it rationally without that awful shuddering fear.

'Have some coffee,' he suggested, and poured it from the pot then tipped her liqueur into it.

'Thanks.' She sniffed the aroma coming from the cup appreciatively and held it in both hands as if for warmth. 'But do you think this will help? Not the coffee—'

He smiled down at her. 'I'm sure it will. If you tell yourself you're not five any more, you're *not* lost and now you know what's behind it, then I think you'll probably be able to nip this phobia in the bud. And you're right—fame is not that easy to handle even without an incident like that buried in your subconscious.'

Skye drank her coffee then leant back. He put his arm around her again. 'You've gone to a lot of trouble, Nick. I don't know how to thank you. Especially after I was so ungracious if not downright horrible earlier.'

'You don't have to thank me. By the way, my mother would be only too happy to help. There are ways—mental exercises, breathing and so on—that *will* help, she says. Promise me you'll go and see her?'

'I...yes, I will. But I already feel a bit liberated.'

He was silent. Skye wondered what he was thinking and was about to ask but she changed her mind, and they sat in silence for a while although her thoughts were busy, but it was a companionable silence.

Then she broke it herself. 'Are you thinking what

I'm thinking, Nick?' She tilted her chin so she could see his eyes.

'Tell me.'

'I'm wondering how much this accounts for—well, you are the one person I've always felt safe with.'

'Until yesterday,' he commented. 'Then even I let you down.'

She bit her lip. 'Was it only yesterday? It feels light years away.'

'Accounts for what, Skye?'

She hesitated. 'Why I wanted more than you— maybe even most men—could give?'

He laid his head back and played with her curls. 'Not most men. Most men would have read you better, Skye.'

'Even when *I* didn't know why I was the way I was?'

'Even then. I'll take you home.'

She was still suffering from this abrupt departure when they stood outside their respective hotel doors.

'Goodnight,' she said uncertainly, and for some ridiculous reason held out her hand for him to shake.

He took it. 'Skye…' He seemed curiously lost for words.

'It's OK, Nick. You've acted above and beyond the cause today. Like a true friend. I'll never forget that.'

'The one problem with all this,' he said very quietly, 'is that I can't seem to let you go just yet.'

Her lips parted.

'Therefore, I intend to fly you home in easy stages,

island-hopping along the way, and we won't go out of our way to avoid anyone.'

'Nick, that's...sweet of you,' she said unsteadily, 'but it's not necessary—'

'Come in for a moment.' He opened his door. 'I don't have any intention of seducing you, Skye.'

She made a strange little sound and spread her hands.

He looked at her quizzically. 'We can't hold a discussion out here.'

'Oh, all right, but you were the one who—'

'I know—broke things off rather abruptly. I've been thinking as we walked home, though.'

She shook her head but walked into his room and dumped her bag on the bed. 'So?' She turned to face him with her arms folded, her expression stern.

He smiled slightly. 'Would it matter if we took a few days off?'

'Just the two of us? Nick, we may not make the ideal married couple but it would be incredibly easy to drift back into a relationship—look what happened to us only yesterday afternoon. And island-hopping, lovely as it sounds, would be most conducive to— well, I may not have to spell *that* out for you.' She eyed him militantly.

'So?' he countered mildly.

'Why are you suggesting we put ourselves under that kind of strain?'

'That is talking from the hip, Skye.' He glanced briefly but meaningfully down her figure. Then, as she stiffened and coloured, he murmured, 'Would it be such a bad idea to rekindle our relationship in the

light of a few revelations? We had so much else going
for us, perhaps we could work out a better deal this
time?'

She sat down on the bed because her legs simply
buckled beneath her.

He looked amused and came to sit beside her on
the end of the bed although not touching her.

She closed her eyes and said barely audibly, 'I laid
us to rest, Nick, on a patch of grass in the starlight,
in front of a winning post. I even dreamt of some
flowers lying there to mark the spot. Don't ask me to
go through that again.'

'I'm sorry. But I didn't know at the time that I
could change.' His voice was deep and even. 'I—'

'Nick,' she interrupted, and put her hand over his,
'this is sympathy talking, and a trace of guilt. But it's
not your fault you didn't know. I went to extraordi-
nary lengths to hide it from you. But I could no more
live with guilt, or sympathy, than I could with…what
happened before. Thank you for offering, all the
same.'

'Skye—'

'Don't say another word.' And she stopped him by
kissing him. Then she stood up.

He did speak. 'I thought about ten o'clock tomorrow morning would be a good time to leave, Skye.
We could get up to Lizard Island easily.'

She froze. 'Haven't you heard a word I said?'

'Oh, yes,' he drawled. 'As you see, I remain un-
convinced. Besides which I promised your mother,
and my mother, that I'd take good care of you over
the next few days in case there's any reaction. Your

mother was especially relieved. She was all set to fly up here, although she has another phobia. She doesn't like flying and she's minus a chef at the moment.'

'I'll—don't count on finding me here tomorrow morning, Nick,' she said through her teeth.

'You'll run away? Skye, that is a little childish,' he reproved gravely. 'The other thing is—you're never going to be hard to find.'

'How I ever imagined I was in love with you, Nick Hunter, is a complete mystery to me,' she marvelled bitterly.

'Well—' he shrugged '—why don't you look at it along those lines?'

'What lines?' she enquired through her teeth.

'You could take this time together to prove to me that you're not.'

Skye came out of the water refreshed the next afternoon, although no wiser as to why she'd decided to take up Nick's challenge. He was lazing on the sand in a pair of maroon board shorts with a straw hat pulled down over his eyes. The flight had been magical as they'd floated over the coast and the reef before he'd touched down, as light as a feather, on the island runway.

Lizard was a big island, with a high rocky peak, and rather bare until you got closer. The resort, a lodge overlooking Anchor Bay, nestled unobtrusively amongst palm trees and her room featured the use of some lovely natural timber. She had her own private balcony and a king-size bed.

Everything was luxurious but low key at the lodge

and they knew how to cater for celebrities because many did come to Lizard, not only for its unspoiled beauty but also its proximity to world-class Black Marlin fishing grounds.

Nick had told her all this on the flight. She'd responded that she knew this, Lizard was famous after all—but had he taken into account that this was island-hopping in the wrong direction for one thing? They were going north, not south, away from Sydney. And, for another, she might have been better off at a place where they didn't ensure their guests' privacy so well.

He'd turned to her with a wicked little smile. 'No one should miss out on Lizard, Skye.'

'It'll have to be quite something to beat Haggerstone,' she'd replied.

'Trust me. See that cape over there?' He'd pointed towards the mainland. 'That's Cape Flattery, so named by Captain Cook because it flattered him into thinking that he'd got out of the reef.'

'Which he hadn't, I take it?'

'No. But they took a long boat to Lizard, which he named after the giant monitor lizards they encountered, and climbed to the peak, and from there he saw the passage through the reef. I'll take you up to Cook's Lookout, Skye.'

She'd stopped herself from saying something irritable and taken refuge in silence. Not that it had appeared to daunt him in the slightest.

It was when she'd taken her one light bag off the plane that she'd stopped again and sighed suddenly.

'What?'

'Even for me, I'm getting tired of these clothes and having to be inventive!'

He'd laughed. 'There's a lovely shop.'

There was and she'd bought herself a new dress in the spirit of—what? she asked herself. Defiance, decadence? It wasn't a cheap dress—nothing was cheap about Lizard—and she didn't actually need a new dress apart from the circumstances—depression, a desire to take her mind off those circumstances? Probably a bit of everything, she decided gloomily.

But it was impossible to emerge from this late afternoon swim, she found, feeling gloomy or depressed. They'd walked over to Watson's Bay where the sand was incredibly fine and white and the water turquoise.

She sat down beside Nick wrapped in her towel and he pushed his hat up then leant up on his elbow. 'Nice?'

'Beautiful. There's a lot of activity here.' She scanned the twenty-odd boats at anchor in the bay and the people on the beach.

'There's a camping ground over there.' He pointed. 'Lizard is not only for the rich and famous although they're kept well away from the resort. It's also one of the great south-easterly anchorages on the way to and from Cape York. Even the navy takes refuge here at times.'

'Oh.'

'And behind us—' he pointed again '—are the remains of Mrs Watson's cottage. This bay is named after her as well as an island in the Howick group further north—'

'I've heard of her,' Skye broke in. 'Didn't she have to sail away in a bathtub or something like that?'

'Well, it was a bit bigger. Her husband was a bêche-de-mer fisherman and while he was away at sea she, her baby and her two Chinese servants were set upon by Aborigines. Mrs Watson, the baby and one servant managed to escape in the tub they used to boil the bêche-de-mer in. They ended up on Watson Island and perished from thirst.'

'That's awfully sad,' Skye said, blinking.

'She kept a diary until the end. It's in the Brisbane Museum with the tub although she's buried in Cooktown—'

'Stop it, Nick,' Skye begged. 'You're making me cry!'

He sat up and put his arm around her. 'I didn't know you were such a softie, Skye.'

She sniffed. 'I don't think you have to be soft to be moved by that. Can you imagine how terrifying it would be to be floating around out there in a tub with a baby?'

He grimaced and kissed the top of her wet head. 'Sorry I told you. What say we go back to the lodge and have a sundowner on one of our balconies?'

'All right.'

She decided to shower and change first so they arranged to meet on her balcony in an hour's time.

She washed her hair and donned her new dress. It was exquisitely simple, in a misty pink, filmy material with swirling silver sequinned flowers. It was straight but with a layered skirt that reached down to a handkerchief point on one side. It went perfectly with her

silver sandals—and would have set off her beautiful
Tanzanite engagement ring perfectly, she found herself thinking before she abruptly cut off those kind of
thoughts.

She was ready when Nick arrived in a pale beige
linen suit and an open-necked olive-green shirt.

'Nice,' she said, as she would have done when they
were engaged. She'd always liked his taste in clothes
which was somewhere between Armani and his father's sombre suits.

'Thank you. Not nearly as nice as you look,' he
murmured. 'What would you like? The same?'

She nodded and drifted out onto the veranda.

He brought her a gin and tonic and a beer for himself. 'The food is also legendary here so prepare yourself. You certainly have gathered plenty of material
for your book.' He sat down opposite, raised his glass
to her and added, 'How's it going?'

Her eyes sparkled. 'It's a mass of uncoordinated
information at the moment. I've got notes everywhere, recipes—it could take a month to get sorted
out.'

'Any plans for after that?'

'No plans for anything yet.' She sipped her drink.
'How about you?'

'I've been ordered home,' he said humorously.
'Pippa is coming from Paris with a fiancé in tow.
They plan to get married here.'

'A Frenchman?'

'Yes, a count.'

Skye's eyes widened. 'You don't say!'

He grimaced. 'There's a certain amount of concern

because he's divorced and quite a bit older. I'm not anticipating this family reunion to be entirely—easy.'

'You poor thing. If I were you I'd go walkabout and commune with your beloved rocks. I have a friend,' she continued, 'who avoids family reunions like the plague although she loves them dearly, but preferably not *en masse*. And I believe weddings can be particularly stressful.' She paused. 'Of course you'd have to go to it! Just steer clear of getting involved in all the arrangement-making.'

Nick laughed. 'I may yet take your advice. I didn't find our wedding plans particularly stressful, however.'

'That's because you left it all to me, my mother and your mother,' Skye said ruefully.

'Should I have taken more of an interest?' he queried, not quite smiling.

'It might have been handy if you'd taken an interest in undoing all the arrangements,' Skye said prosaically. 'Such as sending back the presents, writing all the notes et cetera.'

'I didn't think of that.'

'On the other hand, when you're not talking to someone, let alone hating them—' an imp of humour lit her eyes again '—it would never have worked anyway.'

'Did you—feel you hated me?'

'I wasn't exactly feeling well-disposed towards you, Nick,' she replied with that glint of humour fading. 'I imagine you were feeling the same.'

'True,' he conceded. 'But I wouldn't say I hated you.'

Skye tipped a hand as if to signify a lack of interest. 'It's all water under the bridge now anyway.'

'So it is.' He sat back but continued to study her. 'Think you'll ever go for a wedding with all the trimmings again, Skye?'

She shivered although it was hardly cold. 'I doubt it,' she said lightly, though. 'I may be jinxed in that regard. How about you?'

'I would appear to be jinxed on the subject entirely.'

Skye opened her mouth to query this then decided against it. 'Could we talk about something else?' she asked.

'The weather?' he suggested gravely.

'OK.' The little look she shot him was tinged with satire. 'I guess it gets really hot here midsummer.'

'Yep. Which is not that far away. Guess what? It is time to go to dinner. Think we can be civilized?'

She gazed at him innocently. 'I don't see why not.'

They managed to chat inconsequentially and fairly companionably over dinner, which they chose to eat alfresco on the lodge veranda.

Skye paused once to think that it was going well. That the tension that had blown up over their failed wedding plans had eased and they were friends again. It was her own foolishness that caused it to change...

They walked along the beach after dinner; she took her sandals off and felt fine. Until she stopped to look over the darkened water towards the north and was gripped by a nameless feeling of dread.

'Skye?' He'd walked on but he came back to stand

beside her. 'Something wrong?' He had his jacket slung over one shoulder and his trousers rolled up.

'No, no,' she denied hastily. 'But I think I'd like to go to bed.'

'OK. Let's find somewhere to rinse our feet.'

They did so and before long were standing outside her door. 'Thanks, Nick. G-goodnight,' she said unevenly.

'Not until you tell me what's wrong, Skye,' he insisted quietly.

'I don't know what's wrong! I—' She broke off and bit her lip, not only for admitting anything but because that dark reef-and island-studded water stretching up to Cape York was on her mind. Then comprehension dawned. 'I can't stop thinking about Mrs Watson and her baby lost out there...'

He unlocked her door, picked her up and carried her inside.

'If only I'd never brought it up.' He sat down in a chair with her still in his arms.

'If only I wasn't such an idiot.' She shivered.

'I think it could be that it's come on top of remembering yourself lost, Skye. That's why it's made such an impact, but you're not lost, are you?'

Her dread started to recede as she concentrated on him—the warmth of his body through his shirt, the way his dark hair lay, the blue shadows on his jaw—and finally she closed her eyes with a contented little sigh and fell asleep.

She woke several hours later to find herself in bed in her underwear—a matching set of the palest grey satin camisole and French knickers trimmed with white lace. The bedside lamp was on and Nick was asleep in a chair pulled up beside the bed. She sat up, leaning back on her hands, and his eyes flickered open.

They stared at each other, dark eyes into sky-blue. The sheet had slipped down to her waist and one of the delicate straps of her camisole had slipped down, revealing the swell of her breast.

He didn't move his head but his eyes took in the smooth golden skin of her shoulders and arms then wandered down to the outline of her nipples beneath the supple satin.

He sat up abruptly, reached for his jacket slung over the back of the chair, and went to stand up.

But their eyes locked again, drawn by the power of knowing each other well enough to know there was no way to fight this. No words to say that would make it go away—the powerful effect they had on each other. And Skye didn't move. She didn't try to draw up the sheet or draw up her strap. Until, that was, she sat upright and held out her hand to him. He took it slowly, then his arms were around her waist, and she was cradling his head to her breasts.

They didn't speak—what could you say to a man you loved to make love to but couldn't live with? Skye asked herself once, and closed her eyes in pain.

It wasn't pain they brought to each other, though. It was sheer glory for her as he handled her slim, soft body with consummate skill, freeing her of her underwear, renewing his acquaintance with it and doing to it all the things she loved.

It almost made her dizzy to renew her acquaintance with the planes and angles of his body, to be free to smooth her hands along the sleek muscles of his arms and back and along the width of his shoulders... To be slight in his arms and feel his strength, just there under the surface. To tilt her head back as they sat opposite each other on their heels and close her eyes because she knew what was coming and, even without his hand on her, be taut with anticipation and have that lovely kind of rapture running through her.

She didn't have to wait long. He touched her nipples but they'd already flowered under his gaze alone. Then he kissed them and tantalizingly drew away to trace a path of delight around them with his fingers. She responded by stilling his hand with her own, carrying it to her lips and kissing the palm then offering him her mouth.

He drew her down beside him as they kissed. Then he cupped her hips and she slid her leg between his. It was sheer heaven to press herself against him and to hold him, knowing that the contact was arousing him powerfully. As powerfully as it was making her tremble with need and sheer desire that was so lovely and could only lead to the most exquisite fulfilment.

It was more than exquisite when it came. It was as if they were united in every breath, every tremor, at one with each other in a tangle of sweat-dewed limbs, never to be parted.

But, to break her heart further, she found they could also still laugh together, as, eventually, he pushed her damp hair off her face gently, pulled up the sheet and held her loosely. 'On a scale of one to ten, I don't think we've ever topped that, Skye.'

'Oh, I think that was beyond one to ten; we may even have broken the scale.' She snuggled against him, she couldn't help herself, and they laughed softly, then quietened, and finally fell asleep.

When Nick woke the next morning, she was sitting on the end of the bed, dressed, packed and ready to go.

CHAPTER SIX

HE SAT up, shoved his hair out of his eyes and discovered he was furious. 'What the *hell* do you think you're doing?'

It was no consolation to see her eyes widen with shock. And widen further as he jumped out of bed to stand in front of her stark naked.

'And don't look like that either, Skye,' he heard himself order curtly. 'Not after last night, not to mention all the nights, mornings, afternoons and other strange times we've made love with extreme passion. Isn't it time you grew up a bit? You can't surely be so innocent as you contrive to appear!'

'I don't contrive to appear anything,' she retorted with sudden spirit as she stood up herself. 'But if you want to have any kind of a discussion with me, Nick, put some clothes on!'

He felt himself slip into another gear. 'Why, Skye? Afraid we'll not be able to help ourselves again?' he mocked. 'That is what happened last night if you remember—I hope you're not going to pretend otherwise or wrongly apportion some kind of blame for it.'

She closed her eyes briefly and he saw her swallow. 'No. It was all my fault. I was being morbid and stupid. But don't *you* see?' she said intensely. 'Without poor Mrs Watson and her baby, it would never have happened.'

'Rubbish,' he said through his teeth. 'It would have happened anyhow. It might have taken a bit longer before it happened, that's all.'

'Nick,' she said on a breath, and he watched with a kind of grim fascination as so many expressions chased through her eyes, leading to final comprehension. 'Did you—did you actually plan for this—for something like this…?' She stopped and gestured towards the bed.

'Not last night, no, I didn't plan anything; *you*—'

'I…I know, but is that why you suggested this— this trip?'

'Only you, Skye, would have believed it couldn't or shouldn't have happened. I'm not a block of wood and I'm certainly not as easily manipulated as Bryce Denver. But before you brand me as the ultimate villain,' he said roughly, 'it's not entirely my fault that we can't keep our hands off each other!'

He waited as she absorbed this and knew she would blush. Which she did—another cause for grim satisfaction, he found as that pink tinge beneath her smooth skin ran all the way down her slender neck. He paused to marvel at the fact that he could still make her blush then his mouth hardened because he *still* couldn't work out whether this innocence was something he loved or something that exasperated him mightily.

Skye, seeing that hardening, suddenly decided she'd had enough. She picked up her cap and bag and fled for the door.

He caught her easily enough, picked her up and carried her, kicking and struggling, back to the bed where he sat down with her in his arms. 'Stop it,' he said quietly. 'You must know me well enough by now to know I'm not some kind of monster.'

Skye sat up in his lap and eyed him furiously. 'No, I don't! I don't think I know you at all any more and, Nick, one of our great problems was that we didn't know each other properly.'

'That's why you're determined to run away again?'

'Yes.' She was clipped and severe.

He laughed softly and hugged her briefly. 'All right. Off you go.' He lifted her up with his hands around her waist and set her on her feet. 'I think the first flight comes in around eleven o'clock today.' He got up himself and headed for the shower.

Skye was sitting in an armchair when he came out.

He raised a wry eyebrow at her and started to pull on his trousers.

'It's all very well being superior, Nick,' she said stiffly, 'but this is my room and I might as well wait here.'

'Which you'd forgotten to take into account earlier?' he suggested with some satire.

Skye was silent as she mentally berated herself for sheer stupidity. In fact, when she'd woken and seen how deeply asleep Nick was—he could sleep like a log anywhere—her first impulse had been to just slip away.

Flights et cetera had raised their head with her as she'd showered, dressed and packed, but, perhaps most of all, leaving with no explanation. So she'd decided to wait until he woke, then try and explain things rationally to him. Only to be confronted by a Nick as she'd never seen him before, which *had* prompted a headlong, thoughtless flight.

He reached for his olive-green shirt then came to sit opposite her with it still in his hands. 'When we go, we'll go together, Skye. But you're right—I think we might leave Lizard and Mrs Watson to rest in peace.'

She stared at him and thought involuntarily how beautiful he was. The skin of his shoulders was sleek and tanned, the sprinkling of dark hairs on his chest disappeared beneath his trousers along with a taut, hard diaphragm. The muscles in his arms were smooth and powerful and his wet hair lay flat against a well-shaped head.

All of which—and she swallowed beneath the weight of it—brought back memories of the night before.

Then it struck her that she'd never stopped to wonder whether he was handsome in a conventional sense. There was so much personality in his face together with those often expressive, sometimes enigmatic, always fascinating dark eyes, you had no need to sum him up feature by feature; the whole was simply dynamic. She *had* sometimes marvelled that she, Skye Belmont, could be everything to this man.

As she looked into his eyes now and found them supremely enigmatic, all the old doubts, and some new ones, came back to plague her. How to get through to him, though…?

'I want to go home, Nick,' she said steadily. 'I

thank you very much for all you've done but I'm not convinced there's any reason for us to...try again.'

'That's rather remarkable—I thought we broke the scale last night?' he drawled, and slid his arms into the olive-green cotton.

She watched him button up the shirt fixedly. Anything rather than having to encounter his eyes. 'It probably happens to you all the time.'

'What makes you think that?'

'Well, I'm sure Wynn is capable of a bit of scale-breaking, for example.'

He smiled unexpectedly. 'I have no idea. You're not still worried about Wynn?'

'I...you...no...uh...what do you mean?' This time she looked straight into his eyes without stopping to think, her own a very puzzled blue.

'I didn't sleep with Wynn.'

She blinked. 'But...I mean, you said you consoled each other!'

He shrugged and reached for his socks. 'Emotionally but not physically. I did try to tell you this, Skye,' he added as she looked astounded. 'You gave me to understand you weren't interested.'

'But Wynn herself...' Skye stopped.

'Told you otherwise?'

'No! But she might just have well have shouted it from the nearest treetop.'

'If so, that was only her way of bolstering her ego. Or,' he meditated, 'perhaps you were being super-sensitive?'

'That does it!' Skye stood up decisively. 'I've had

enough insults from you this morning, Nick Hunter!
I'm going to breakfast.'

He slid his shoes on, raked his fingers through his
hair and said sweetly, 'Me too—I could eat a horse.
Fantastic sex always did have that effect on me.
Which was why you were such a delight to know,
Skye.'

She wasn't sure whether she growled audibly but
she certainly felt like it.

How do you break through a brick wall? she wondered as they lingered over coffee.

It was a hot, clear day and they'd eaten their breakfast with only the most mundane conversation between them.

Then he said, 'Would you like another swim before
we take off?'

'Take off for where?' she asked cautiously.

'We're a long way from home; we'll have to break
it up a bit—Great Keppel?'

'No, the mainland somewhere, Nick, or not at all.'

'Mackay, Rockhampton, Gladstone?' He eyed her
wickedly. 'Not terribly exciting, Skye.'

'I've had enough excitement to last me for a while.'
Her tone was slightly bitter.

'Skye...' he paused and looked out over Anchor
Bay '...I don't think I've told anyone this but the
prospect of stepping into my father's shoes has never
entirely appealed to me.'

She put her cup down carefully and frowned at
him. 'What do you mean?'

'He's talking about relinquishing the reins com-

pletely and going to live on an island. Once he gets
Pippa sorted out, that is.'

'But—you would have known this was coming,
wouldn't you?'

He gestured. 'Some time in the future, naturally.
Not as actual reality, though. And it doesn't mean to
say I relish it.'

'Why not?'

'It's an awful lot of responsibility.'

'Do you mean you wouldn't be able to go away
and do your own thing?' she asked as a little window
seemed to open in her mind so that she frowned suddenly. 'You'd be really tied down...'

He shrugged. 'Well, put it this way, to get where
he got, my father made it his whole life. To take it
on to the next century could require the same dedi-
cation. I don't know whether I—have that dedica-
tion.'

'I've seen you in your office,' she said slowly.
'You—can look like the ultimate tycoon, you sound
like one when you're not—' She stopped and bit her
lip.

'Making love to you?' he murmured wickedly.

She absolutely refused to blush this time although
he had, on one occasion, locked the door of his office,
told Florence via the phone that he wasn't to be dis-
turbed under any circumstances, and done just that on
the broad, comfortable settee.

To Skye's relief, when she'd come down from the
cloud nine he'd elevated her to, it had been long past
five o'clock and everyone else had gone home, including Flo. Even so, she'd taken advantage of the

luxurious bathroom attached to his office suite, so she could leave the building at least feeling as if she looked normal.

'Heady days, those were,' she commented as she sat on the veranda of Lizard Island lodge, refusing to be discomposed.

'As you say,' he replied a shade dryly.

'Why are you telling me this now, Nick?'

'I thought it might give you a new insight into me, that's all.'

'I don't see how it could affect us—'

'But you have told me that one of our big problems was how little we really knew each other,' he countered.

She sat back, feeling confused. 'True, but that's all the more reason for you not to want to be pinned down by a wife. Look at it this way: if you do step into your father's shoes, there'll be even less time for a wife—from what you've told me. And if you don't, although I can't visualize that, Nick,' she said honestly, 'you'd be free to roam the world doing other things.'

He looked wry. 'It's quite a dilemma.'

She sat up and put her elbows on the table. 'I wish I could help. I mean on a friendship level,' she said with a frown. 'Have you discussed this *with* your father?'

'No.' He shrugged. 'It's always been his greatest wish that I do take over.'

She paused to think about Nick's father. She'd liked him. He was unostentatious although a stickler for propriety and it wasn't hard to see that he lived and breathed his minerals empire.

Perhaps, it occurred to her, and her eyes widened, Nick's mother had pursued her own career as much as she had in a form of self-defence against a man who was rarely there, as for any other reason. Was *that* why his mother had worried about what she, Skye, was getting herself into? Could it be a case of like father, like son in their own different ways?

Could Nick himself have been conditioned by his parents' marriage to expect something similar from his own wife?

'Skye?'

She blinked and Nick came into focus again. She bit her lip and said hesitantly, 'Maybe your father is more intuitive than you give him credit for?'

'I doubt it if he's considering burying himself on an island,' he said impatiently.

'It doesn't sound like him, though.' She wrinkled her brow. 'It might be a test to see how it does appeal to you. Even on an island, in this day and age he'd be able to keep in touch.'

Nick looked at her with sudden amusement. 'By the way, he was extremely annoyed with me for letting you slip through my fingers. I can't help wondering—' he frowned slightly '—whether the two have anything to do with each other.'

'As in how?'

'As in pointing out to me that it's about time I settled down,' he said somewhat dryly.

'That would be the last reason you should get married for, Nick,' she said thoughtfully.

'Perhaps,' he conceded, then stood up abruptly. 'OK, let's shake the dust of Lizard from our shoes.'

'Where?' she asked as they took off.

'Brisbane,' he replied briefly.

'But I thought…'

'We'll land at Rocky to refuel. We should make Brisbane before it's dark.'

She glanced at him. He had earphones and a mike on and there was something unusually uncompromising in the set of his mouth. 'Nick,' she said tentatively, 'I feel as if I've let you down.'

His dark eyes were penetrating as he glanced at her briefly but he only said casually, 'Not at all, Skye.'

'I mean I *really* wish I could help, especially after the way you helped me, but getting back together could only compound the problem, don't you think?'

'There's only one valid reason for us to get back together, Skye, and that would be if we found we couldn't live apart.'

'Well, I agree absolutely—'

He laughed softly and not entirely pleasantly. 'I knew you'd say that.'

She flinched. He saw it and shrugged. 'Look, don't worry about it. There is an alternative.'

She stared at him with her lips parted as her mind raced.

'You could connect up with a commercial flight at Hamilton Island if you preferred. You'd get to Sydney in one hop by tonight.'

It was like a blow over the region of her heart and it must have shown in her expression because he said cynically, 'What were you expecting, Skye? That I suggested we forget about getting married and just resume intimate relations? As we did last night,' he added pointedly.

She licked her lips and wondered desperately what she had expected. 'No. Uh…I guess it *was* like having the door slammed in my face but…but then I obviously can't help,' she said barely audibly. Then she decided to be hanged for a sheep. 'Nor was Hamilton Island the most tactful suggestion.'

'Because of Wynn? And the fact that I may be tempted to break the scale with her?' he drawled.

'Possibly,' she agreed tautly. 'However, you go ahead and do what you like. I will go home in one hop!'

'Skye—Hamilton Island happens to be handy and have a lot of flights—'

'I'm not a fool, Nick. So does Mackay, Rockhampton, Gladstone—'

'Yes, but they're all further on than Hamilton and in this state of—war mightn't it be a good idea to curtail this encounter?' he shot back.

'You're the one who declared this war!'

'No, Skye, you're the one who invited me to sleep with her last night then got up and packed her bags this morning.'

'Well, I'm glad I did,' she said proudly. 'There was always an unfinished kind of aura about our affair, Nick. Now I've done that, I've said a last goodbye. So take me to Hamilton; I really can't wait to get home.'

He did just that.

There was not a tear in her eye as they floated over the Whitsundays in a strained silence and landed on the island. Nor when she said goodbye formally to him after he'd insisted on organizing her flight for her—fortunately she only had a twenty-minute wait. They were like two strangers, and his dark eyes were hard and cool.

He said as she was about to board the jet, 'Take care, Skye. And don't forget to go and see my mother.'

'I won't. You too. Goodbye, Nick.' And she turned away without waiting for his reply. Nor did her composure crack, not even as she walked through the terminal at Sydney and realized she didn't give a damn who recognized her and she'd taken no precautions against it.

Then she saw her mother coming towards her with open arms.

'Mum!' They hugged. 'What are you doing here?'

'Nick rang me,' Iris Belmont explained. 'He said…he… Oh, Skye, my darling, don't cry…'

'I'm better, Mum. Promise,' Skye said as they ate dinner in the restaurant. She'd told her mother almost everything, more than she'd ever told her before.

The restaurant was closed, actually, but it had been a busy evening and Skye had been only too happy to help out. Iris was still minus a chef.

'But—' her mother hesitated '—you don't think he might have been right? You did seem to have an awful lot going for you.'

Skye looked at her mother affectionately. 'I think

you might have been right. There's a lot more to Nick than appears on the surface. But one thing he's not right about—he can't call all the shots—when he feels like it.'

Unbeknownst to Skye, Iris decided wisely not to pursue the subject. She said instead, 'I wish you'd told me how you felt about crowds!'

Skye grimaced. 'So do I but I didn't want to worry you, and I hadn't really realized that it was growing, I guess. But that may be a thing of the past now too.'

'You will go and see Margaret Hunter, though?' Iris stared at her anxiously. 'I spoke to her and she doesn't think you should just let it lie and assume it's all over.'

Skye sighed. 'Perhaps another—'

'Oh, Skye,' her mother entreated, 'please. I have such faith in her!'

'Mum, it's difficult,' Skye protested, and was astonished to see sudden tears in her mother's eyes.

'The thing is,' Iris said intensely, 'she also knows my side of the story. We had quite a long chat.'

'Oh—all right,' Skye conceded. 'I'll give it a few days, though.'

'You will not, Skye Belmont.' Her mother rose and reached for the phone. 'You'll do it tomorrow!'

In the event, Skye was more than happy to confide in someone the next day, because she was not only furious but also not at all sure she could handle fame ever again.

She'd woken to find herself splashed all over the front page of a morning newspaper. She'd been snapped with Nick in Cairns, snapped at Lizard, snapped in the airport lounge on Hamilton Island and, most devastating of all, snapped, obviously in tears, with her mother at Sydney airport. *Why was Skye crying?* the caption asked. *Did her reunion with Nick Hunter fall flat?*

'I can't believe it! I hate it,' she said passionately to Margaret Hunter in her pleasant consulting room, pointing to the paper.

'My dear—' Nick's mother was small, slim and grey-haired but she had his dark eyes '—I know it's awful but you have to learn to live with it.'

'Tell me how,' Skye pleaded desperately. 'Nick said wanting to disguise myself was not...normal, but surely anything that avoids this has to be plain common sense!'

'There are two separate issues here, Skye,' Margaret said gently. 'An invasion of your privacy which, quite justifiably, has made you hopping mad. But that's not the same thing as a morbid fear of crowds.'

Skye subsided.

'How...is Nick?' Margaret asked tentatively then, as if she'd been in two minds about asking.

'Fine—uh—' Skye paused to study the woman who was to have been her mother-in-law and couldn't help but observe that she was troubled. 'Haven't you—? You sound as if you don't—know.'

Margaret grimaced. 'Nick and his father had an almighty row over him breaking up with you, Skye. We haven't seen him since.'

'You mean no contact at all?' Skye asked, wide-eyed.

'Oh, I've spoken to him on the phone. And I gather his father has as well but—' she sighed '—things are very strained. On top of it, Richard is talking about retiring—I mean really retiring—and I don't know— I just don't know how Nick feels about it.'

'You poor thing,' Skye said involuntarily. 'You're probably caught in the middle?' She raised an enquiring eyebrow.

Margaret nodded ruefully. 'Also, Pippa is coming home with a divorced French count she wants to marry who is years older than she is.'

'Nick told me.' Skye sat back and opened her hands in a gesture of sympathy.

'So you and Nick are not…?' Margaret hesitated.

'We're not getting back together, no. He was wonderful,' Skye said intensely, 'About *this* business, and he did suggest we try again, but only after he found out about the claustrophobia. I couldn't—do it. It nearly killed me to know that he wasn't even that keen on us having children the first time around, so, I think I may always love him, but…' She stopped and sighed.

'There's a part of Nick you don't think you can ever get to?'

'Yes,' Skye said sadly.

Margaret was silent for a good minute. Then she said slowly, 'I've often wondered whether it's a reaction in Nick to this thing that's been hanging over his head for so long. This sort of inevitability that he was one day going to have to step into his father's shoes.'

Skye sat transfixed.

'Don't get me wrong—it's not as if he hates his father for it. In so many ways they're two of a kind. They have that sort of business flair, that acumen and vision, and if it had been his own creation Nick may have felt just as dedicated, but...'

'But that's why, ultimately, he's so averse to being tied down in any way? Because he's always felt the weight of this?' Skye offered.

'Precisely.' Margaret shrugged.

'I've thought of that. He told me only yesterday that he wasn't sure about stepping into his father's shoes. I...well, I stopped to wonder how *you* had coped. Because each of them in their own way is...hard to reach, I would imagine.'

'It came down to one simple thing in the end,' Margaret said slowly. 'I was more miserable away from Richard than I was with him, even fighting for recognition as his soul mate. So I stopped fighting and took another approach. I did my own thing.'

'Have you been happy?' Skye whispered.

'Not all the time, no,' Margaret conceded. 'But, when I have, I've been happier than I could have been with anyone else on earth.'

Skye blinked several times. 'I don't know if I have the fortitude you have,' she said huskily. 'I just don't know.'

'There is another way of looking at it,' Margaret said thoughtfully, 'and I'm wondering whether Richard may have divined all this and that's why he's decided to get out now. Once he leaves it will be Nick's creation, to take it on anyway. So instead of a weight hanging over his head he may feel liberated and, well, less prone to wanting to escape.'

'Have you—forgive me, I don't mean to be incredibly personal—but have you asked Mr Hunter if that's why he wants to retire?'

'Men,' Margaret Hunter said with sudden bitterness, 'can be impossible at times, Skye. Since this row between Nick and his father, every time I try to bring anything up in the context of Nick, Richard accuses me of siding with him.'

'Oh, dear. Have I caused that much strife?' Skye looked genuinely conscience-stricken.

Margaret laughed. 'You're very sweet, Skye. No— not that we don't love you and, to be honest, thought you were very right for him, but I think this conflagration was waiting to happen anyway. Skye, should we discuss crowds now?'

Skye went to the restaurant after her time with Margaret Hunter, where her mother was waiting eagerly.

'How did it go?'

'She was very helpful,' Skye said, but slowly.

'You don't look—' Iris hesitated '—that much helped, darling.'

Skye made an effort to drag her mind from all the revelations of the morning that had nothing to do with her fear of crowds and set about trying to reassure her mother. 'You wait and see. There's a new me under this old exterior, Mum. I don't suppose you've acquired a new chef during the course of this morning?'

'No! I've interviewed three but not one of them is suitable!'

Skye hugged her. 'Just as well you've got me, then, isn't it?'

The restaurant proved to be a lifeline during the next weeks.

And during the day Skye concentrated on her book. This wasn't as easy, though, because so much of her new material reminded her of Nick and she often found herself sitting with her chin propped on her hands, wondering what she'd turned her back on, wondering why she felt as if she'd let him down, wondering if she could be a version of his mother...

Then they met and it could hardly have been less auspicious.

'We've got an absolutely full house tonight including a party of eight,' Iris said anxiously. 'Think you can cope? I don't know why there's this dearth of good chefs!'

'Of course,' Skye said serenely. 'And people are probably holding onto their good staff because Christmas is not that far away—but perhaps it's an idea to cut the menu down slightly?'

'Good thinking,' Iris applauded, and walked over to the menu board armed with a duster and a piece of chalk.

The evening started well but at eight o'clock Iris walked into the kitchen looking shell-shocked.

'What?' Skye asked as she stirred a béchamel sauce and grilled an eye fillet at the same time.

'You're not going to believe this but Nick and Pippa are amongst the party of eight!'

Skye froze then continued what she was doing automatically. 'So?'

'He said…he said he didn't know which restaurant had been booked until he arrived. Neither did Pippa; someone else made the booking and gave them a lift.'

'Mum, there's nothing we can do about it.'

'No, no, of course not. But I didn't tell him you were right here in the kitchen when he asked after you. I just said you were fine as if you were somewhere else.'

'Then all I've got to do is stay out of sight. Here.' Skye handed her mother two plates. 'Look, don't worry about it. It makes no difference whether I'm here or not or whether he knows or not.'

'He's with that woman, though,' Iris said tragically. 'The one you told me about—didn't you say her name was Mortimer? That's the name the booking was made in, only I just didn't connect the two!'

Skye set her teeth and could have killed herself for the way her hackles rose automatically. But she said calmly, 'It still doesn't matter, Mum. Let's just— carry on. They're getting cold, by the way.'

Iris looked down at the plates in her hands as if she'd never seen them before then dashed out.

Things went smoothly until about ten-thirty—as smoothly as could be expected of a kitchen with a full restaurant to feed. Then they took a turn for the unexpected.

A Frenchman invaded the kitchen as Skye was taking a breather, having dished up the last dessert. Invaded it, what was more, saying, 'I have to meet the chef! I have to toast him, buy him a drink and possibly lure him to France to cook for me. *Oui!* Don't say—' he looked around '—you are he, *mademoiselle*?'

'I am he, *monsieur*, but—' Skye got no further as she was picked up and carried out of the kitchen, to be set down triumphantly before the party of eight!

'It's a she, not a he, Pippa!' the Frenchman marvelled. 'You wouldn't credit it, would you?'

There was a sudden deathly silence until Pippa said on a sigh, 'Oh, yes, I would. So that's why the food was so marvellous—Skye, I'm sorry but we didn't *know* we were coming here or that you were here.'

'Although we should have guessed,' Nick said quietly, and he stood up.

'What's this? Give the girl a drink.' The Frenchman put a glass of champagne into Skye's hands and pulled up a chair for her. 'You *know* my fiancée, Pippa? How fortuitous. She may be able to persuade you to come to France. I assure you our kitchen is of the most modern, the servants' quarters are—'

It was Wynn who broke in. 'Jean-Claude,' she said lightly, 'you're putting your foot in your mouth, *chéri*. This is just about the most famous chef in Australia—not that she looks it right at the moment.' And she let her dark eyes drift down from Skye's chef's hat, the red bandanna tied at her throat to her stained apron over a white shirt and trousers and white gum boots.

Wynn herself was extremely stylish in a caramel silk knit dress that exposed a lot of smooth, tanned skin, and her hair was straight and smooth and flowed like a dark river down her back.

Skye pulled her apron off then her hat, clamped her hand around her glass of champagne and sat down.

'Jean-Claude, if I may call you that,' she said to Pippa's fiancé, 'you're very sweet and it was a natural mistake. I'm only glad that you enjoyed my cooking. Oh, may I introduce my mother? I'm sure she'd enjoy a glass too.' She beckoned to Iris, standing transfixed behind the till.

'I really didn't know we were coming here,' Nick said quietly to her a bit later when everyone was talking to everyone else. 'Or that you'd be cooking. I thought you'd given it up.'

'I'm helping out. Mum is still short-handed. But it doesn't matter, Nick. Please don't avoid the place on my account.' She managed to look comically rueful. 'Restaurants can live or die on such little things. So, Hamilton Island lived up to all expectations, I gather?'

He studied her for a long moment—the flush in her cheeks, her damp curls, the steely little glint in her blue eyes. 'Do you really care one way or the other, Skye?'

Her gaze didn't waver for a long moment then she grimaced. 'You're a little hard to work out some-times, Nick, I guess, but then you always were! I hope

Wynn knows what she's in for.' She drained her glass and set it down gently.

Whereupon he turned to Wynn and drawled, 'I guess we should get this party on the road, my sweet.'

CHAPTER SEVEN

'AND what's more we're going to the wedding,' Skye said to her mother. 'I quite liked Pippa's count even though he's been divorced, and he's not *that* much older. Besides, how could you refuse such a charming invitation?'

'Skye,' Iris said warningly, 'you're in a dangerous mood.'

'I know.' Skye shrugged. 'Just kidding. About the wedding, I mean.'

It was the next morning and a beautifully embossed wedding invitation had just been hand-delivered as Jean-Claude had promised faithfully it would be as he'd left the night before. He had obviously been unaware of Skye's engagement to his soon-to-be brother-in-law or of any of the tensions that had flowed around the table.

Skye was having coffee with her mother in her own flat—a converted loft in an old house on the harbour now divided into flats. It was spacious, airy and had lovely views. It was also home to Skye's minimalist decorating and magnificent collection of indoor plants.

'Didn't you tell me there was likely to be no wedding?' Iris continued.

'Jean-Claude, *chérie*—' Skye used an exaggerated French accent '— must have won his in-laws over.

And they're certainly wasting no time. It's next week.' She studied the card, thinking of her own wedding invitations, then put it down.

'When you've got the money they've got, you can organize things in a flash. However, there could be another reason.'

Skye raised an eyebrow at her mother over her coffee cup.

'Pippa could be pregnant.' Iris shrugged. 'Don't ask me how I know; I don't really; I just have this intuition. She had a—certain, rather vulnerable look about her.'

Skye put her cup down slowly. 'Oh, dear. I wonder how Mr Hunter has taken that?'

She was to find out that same day because Pippa came to see her early in the afternoon.

'Why, Pip! Come in.' Skye opened her flat door wide. 'This is a surprise.'

'Skye, I know we never got to know each other that well but I need to talk to you,' Nick's sister said somewhat distraughtly.

Unlike Nick, Pippa was blonde and blue-eyed, but she did have his tall, lean grace and she was supremely elegant even in casual trousers and a shirt.

Skye installed her in an armchair, brought her a cup of tea and a piece of fruit cake. 'What is it?' she asked, sitting down with her own tea.

'Everything,' Pippa said tragically. 'Dad and Nick are in the middle of some kind of deadly battle, Mum is beside herself, I'm pregnant, which Dad doesn't approve of at all, and Jean-Claude is beginning to wonder what he's got himself into. And *everywhere* I turn I'm falling over Wynn!'

'I thought you and Wynn were best friends?'

'We were once—well, we still are,' Pippa said shortly. 'What we were never destined to be was sisters-in-law because she is not the right one for Nick! The thing is, Skye, *you* were, and that's one of the reasons Dad is so mad. Is there no way you and Nick could...? Are you not the least little bit in love with him?'

Skye put her cup down carefully. 'Pip, no...' She stopped and sighed. 'We...we wouldn't be right for each other. I want more than Nick can give so...' She gestured a little hopelessly.

'Skye, could you at least do me one favour? If Dad were at least to think you and Nick might be reconsidering things, it might put him in a better mood.'

'But...'

'I didn't think I'd be like this,' Pippa said. 'Maybe it's because of my baby, but I want my family to be together and in accord on my wedding day. I want them to accept Jean-Claude because he happens to be the *right* man for me despite his previous marriage and being fifteen years older. I don't want this awful feud to spoil things!'

Skye stood up. 'Pippa, look, I would love to be able to help, but do you really know what you're asking?'

'Just come to this formal dinner Mum and Dad are giving tomorrow night—please, Skye,' Pippa begged. 'Even if you just sit next to Nick—and that's *all* I'm asking—it might make Dad stop and think.'

'With Wynn on his other side?' Skye suggested with some irony.

'Wynn's out of town for the next week on a modelling assignment, thank heavens,' Pippa said fervently. 'But they're not—well, I get the feeling Wynn is forcing herself on Nick, anyway.'

'Do you honestly think Nick can't defend himself if he wants to?' This time Skye was outright cynical.

'She's going to be my only bridesmaid. Nick is the best man; it's not that simple, Skye!' Pippa paused. 'It was all arranged before I realized what was going on. The other thing is, you get on well with Jean-Claude! I'll put him on *your* other side. That might also make Dad stop and think that he's not so...so *French*.'

Pippa stopped and they smiled suddenly at each other.

Skye said slowly then, 'Do you honestly think me getting on well with Jean-Claude is going to make the slightest difference to what your father thinks of him?'

Pippa gestured eloquently. 'It just might. He adored you, Skye. And I'm at my wits' end.'

Skye digested this with a frown. Then she said, still looking confused, 'But—what will you tell Nick?'

Pippa stood up and came over to take Skye's hands in her own. 'I won't. There are times when it's no good telling men anything. Please, Skye.' There were tears in the other girl's eyes. 'Look, you may not know this because you've only got your mother but families can be sheer hell!'

*   *   *

As she dressed the next evening, Skye still couldn't believe she'd agreed to do as Pippa asked even though she'd discussed it with her mother and Iris had been of the opinion she should go to the dinner.

Was it because Nick's sister was pregnant? she asked herself. And obviously in an awful state—bad enough to be clutching at wild straws? Was it because of a family in crisis?

All the same, it was a charade she was about to participate in, a sham, even if all she had to do was sit next to Nick, and it didn't sit easily with her.

No, she told herself determinedly, I will not actually connive to let Mr Hunter think I'm going back to Nick. The most I'll do is try to be relaxed and easy in his company. And Jean-Claude's!

She chose a black silk tulle dress with diagonal bands of sequins running round it. It hugged her figure, cupped her breasts and was strapless. It was long and she wore high black shoes with it but no jewellery other than a diamanté butterfly slide in her hair which she left loose otherwise.

But the butterfly might just as well have been in her stomach as she drove up to the Hunter mansion in a cab. Situated at Double Bay, it was not only large and stately, it had a magnificent terraced garden that ran down to the harbour.

The garden was alight with fairy lights and the dinner had been set up on the main terrace outside the house, taking advantage of a fine, warm night.

It was Margaret Hunter who greeted Skye and said that Pippa had confided in her, and told her how grateful she was that Skye had agreed to do something that must be extremely awkward if not actually painful for her.

'I...I'm not going to tell any lies,' Skye stammered as she saw Mr Hunter approaching. 'But I don't see why Nick and I can't look as if we're friends at least—'

'Of course!' Margaret agreed warmly, and turned to her husband. 'I think you know this young lady, Richard!'

Richard Hunter looked supremely surprised then delighted. 'You didn't tell me you'd invited Skye!'

'Do I ever bother you with guest lists?' his wife murmured.

He grimaced. 'No. My dear Skye, I'm so pleased to see you, and does this mean—'

'Richard, they've agreed to be friends,' Margaret interrupted with a delicate little shrug. 'Let's not—'

'Not at all!' It was his turn to break in. 'I shall be the soul of discretion, you may rely on me, but this is very good news...'

Skye escaped as more guests arrived, feeling dreadful. She wandered to the edge of the terrace to discover that a string quartet was playing Mozart on the terrace below. She watched for a moment, unable to help her thoughts escaping to another terrace down the garden that contained a swimming pool and a big tree...then turned at a sound behind her.

It was Nick. Nick, looking darkly handsome in a dinner suit and a snowy shirt but with a blaze of sheer anger in his eyes.

So much so, she literally felt scorched and pinned to the terrace wall as he then proceeded to undress her with his eyes so that she might as well have been standing there in her black silk and lace panties, her tiny girdle and long sheer stockings, which was all she wore under her dress.

In fact so savagely intimate were his dark eyes as they lingered on parts of her figure that he knew so well, she crossed her hands defensively over her breasts in a reflex gesture.

He looked back into her eyes with a glint of sheer mockery. 'What the hell are you doing here, then, Skye, if it's not to torment me with the remembered delights of your body?'

She gasped. 'No! I mean, that's *not* why I'm here!'

He shoved his hands into his pockets. 'Perhaps you should have dressed up a bit more,' he suggested sardonically.

Her hands fell to her sides. 'That's ridiculous, Nick.'

He raised an eyebrow at her and he could hardly have looked more satanic and devastatingly masculine at the same time. 'Go on, then. Why are you here and why am I the last to know it?'

She clenched her fists. He noticed it and looked back into her eyes with cool, hateful amusement.

'I'm only here because of your sister,' she said through her teeth. 'She begged me to come because she thought it might lessen the crisis-ridden state of affairs you and your father are subjecting her to.'

He frowned. 'It's not my fault she's pregnant before the wedding and marrying a Frenchman. I don't see what you can do about it either.'

'That is so like a man, Nick,' she shot back.

'Haven't you stopped to think what she may be going through? Or are you so taken up with fighting your father you haven't even noticed?'

'The only reason I'm fighting my father is because he won't let go of this notion that I should get down on my knees and beg you to come back, Skye. Why don't *you* explain things to him?' he suggested roughly. 'Then we all might get some peace and sanity round here.'

Pippa came up at this point, took one look at her brother's features which might have been cast in iron, and at Skye's pale face, and said despairingly, 'Oh, Nick, if you could just be friends for a night Dad might…it might make some difference!'

Nick transferred his dark gaze to his sister, clad in a gold, off-the-shoulder gown with a bouffant skirt. She looked beautiful, and there was no sign of her pregnancy, but there were faint dark circles under her eyes.

And Skye discovered she was holding her breath as his expression didn't change for a long moment, then softened suddenly. He put his arm around his sister's waist and kissed her brow affectionately. 'Sorry, Pip. I've been—thoughtless. Let's see what we can do to rectify things.'

'You didn't have to go this far,' Skye said, sotto voce but with undeniable feeling as they sat down to dinner.

Nick hadn't left her side during the preceding hour. He'd introduced her to people she hadn't met, calmly ignoring the looks of surprise they'd been unable to hide, and, while he hadn't been precisely lover-like, he had managed to convey subtly that they were a couple. The only thing he'd avoided was any close contact with his father.

'No?' He raised an eyebrow wryly at her. 'You think some tame half-measures are going to achieve anything? My father and I may not be in accord at the moment but one thing I do know—he's not a fool. Do you know why he got all het up again over you, Skye?'

She blinked at him.

'Like the rest of the world,' he drawled, 'he saw the pictures in the paper. Like the rest of the world,' he said with suave satire, 'he was convinced I'd caused you to be crying, heartless monster that I am.'

'You…' She stopped and bit her lip.

'I did make you cry? Or I'm not a heartless monster?' He waited, but when she said nothing more he continued meditatively, 'Have you stopped to think what you've done to my reputation, incidentally?'

Skye unfurled a rose-pink damask napkin and laid it carefully on her lap. 'If anything, women will find you more irresistible, Nick, so I wouldn't worry about it if I were you.'

'But not my father. Nor most other men who are all secretly a little in love with you, Skye. And I don't know about the women either—you're almost a national treasure.'

Skye said something unprintable beneath her breath, causing him to look wickedly amused for a moment. Then she turned pointedly to Jean-Claude.

The sixty or so guests were seated at four round

tables with magnificent floral centrepieces of pink and white roses. The silver cutlery gleamed, the crystal shone, the waiters and waitresses wore black and white, and a moon was rising.

Margaret and Richard Hunter were not at their table, for which Skye gave devout thanks. All the same the tables weren't that far apart and she knew she was visible from most angles. Added to this, the guests had been mixed so that there were people of an age group that made them friends of the Hunter Seniors at Skye's table. Pippa was on the other side of Jean-Claude.

It was as Skye exchanged glances with her across him that it occurred to her that if she could get at least one thing right tonight it would be to take the Frenchman under her wing.

She shook herself mentally as soon as the thought occurred to her. This was a middle-aged count! What could she do to make him more acceptable to Pippa's family and friends?

Treat him as if he were on one of your shows, an inner voice prompted suddenly. You obviously have cuisine in common too. Work on that!

She did. The result was delightful. The rapport between her and Jean-Claude seemed to get the rest of the table going; she could see Pippa relaxing and finally she could sit back feeling as if she'd launched him successfully.

'Masterly,' Nick said dryly. 'I gather that was Skye Belmont, TV personality at work?'

'Yes,' she agreed shortly, and added defiantly, 'I like him but the real criterion is—Pippa loves him.'

'I stand reproved,' he commented.

Skye didn't answer and presently he began to talk to her more normally. She would have given anything to be able to freeze him off or simply ignore him but, apart from the obvious reasons not to, he was diabolically clever about it. Without her quite knowing how, he got her to discuss next year's show and the innovations that were planned for it.

'You know all my pot plants?'

'I do,' he agreed. 'Although not by name.'

Skye grinned. 'Well, you may not know that I grow a lot of herbs as well, so we're going to feature one fresh herb a week—how to grow it, how to use it, how to dry it et cetera. And—' she wrinkled her nose '—I'm not so sure about this one, but we're going to tour some farmyards.'

'Why not sure about that?'

'I think I may be expected to show a rapport with live chickens, pigs and things.'

He laughed. 'If you could see your face!'

She laughed back at him. 'I can imagine it. Not that I have any phobias about chooks and pigs but I haven't ever been closely associated with them!'

He sobered. 'How's it going—phobia-wise, Skye?'

'I haven't really had a chance to test it but I don't worry nearly so much about going to supermarkets and things like that.'

'I'm so glad,' he said gently, and put his hand over hers briefly.

Neither of them was aware that Richard Hunter was watching them closely.

Things didn't stay as serene, however. Nor did

Skye realize that, despite being so nice to her, Nick was still angry underneath…

After dinner, the quartet retired and a band took over. Pippa and Jean-Claude rose and stepped onto the circular dance floor that had been laid down.

'Oh, *no*!' Skye muttered.

'You didn't expect this or you still have painful memories of Bryce?' Nick queried as he stood up and held his hand down to her. 'Believe me, we dance together like a dream, Skye. Or had you forgotten?' For a moment his dark eyes gleamed as a tiger's might. Lazy now but with a hint of ever present danger.

Skye cursed herself inwardly for not having thought about this, and took his hand.

'Nothing's changed,' he remarked as they circled the floor in perfect step with each other. 'Did he write?'

'Bryce? Yes. He also sent me some marvellous photos of Haggerstone and Mount Gregory.'

'How's it going with Maggie?'

'He didn't say. I don't know whether that's good news or not.'

'You wouldn't be having second thoughts about him?'

She looked him straight in the eye. 'As you apparently had about Wynn? Of course not but I liked him, he was a good friend in a time of need, and I felt so sorry for him when he crashed.'

'So did we all,' he murmured. 'You were both rather sweet, swirling your way through the water.'

He stopped dancing as the music changed and then drew her closer into his arms.

'Nick—' Skye swallowed as her heart started to beat differently '—we don't have to do this…'

'You think not?' His dark eyes were ironic and they drifted almost absently along the smooth curves of her shoulders.

'You know, I can't work out why you bother to be nice to me then—like this,' she said bitterly. 'Why would I think otherwise?'

'Because there's a tell-tale little pulse beating rather rapidly at the base of your throat, Skye. I've often watched it although you may have been unaware of me doing so. I know, for example, that I can actually get it to beat faster simply by doing this.'

He released her hand and put both of his on her back, one sliding down to her hips, the other on her skin just above the top of her zip. And he drew her towards him so that he could say the rest of what he was saying into her hair.

'In days gone by, now would be when we'd leave. And either at your place or mine there would be no dress, however lovely, between us, to hinder me touching your breasts just as you like me to, Skye.'

She stumbled but he gathered her smoothly into the beat again, although he moved her a little away and took her hand again so he could look into her eyes as they danced on.

'Did you know,' he continued, his gaze lingering on that pulse at the base of her throat, 'you have a way of tilting back your head, Skye, and closing your eyes that tells me just how much you're loving every damn thing I'm doing to you?'

'Stop it,' she whispered raggedly.

'Why? If it's getting to be too much for you perhaps we should do something about it? Think how happy it would make my father if we disappeared— together. Is that not the game we're playing at the moment?'

'I am going, right now. Nick!' she protested as he pulled her close again.

'Oh, no, Skye,' he said, his body hard and strong against hers, his arms like steel. 'When we slip away, which we'll do shortly, it will be together. You started this.'

'Nick—I didn't know you could be like this!'

He smiled into her eyes and kissed her lightly on the mouth. 'Perhaps you'll think twice before you play with matches again, Skye.'

To her disbelief, he engineered their leaving the party discreetly not long afterwards, although she had his finger marks on her wrist to testify as to how he'd done it. And she was shaking with anger as she sat beside him in a dark green Jaguar as they drove towards her flat.

'Don't imagine you're going to force your way in with me, Nick Hunter!' she warned furiously. 'Talk about a Dr Jekyll and a Mr Hyde. I had no idea what a lucky escape I had when I broke it off with you!'

He grimaced. 'What would you rather have done? Gone on proving to the world we're back together?

That party won't break up until midnight at least and more likely two a.m.'

'You didn't *have* to—we didn't have to—'

'We've been through that before, Skye,' he said impatiently. 'If we're to get my father into a better frame of mind so that Pippa can get to the altar happily, we needed to make it look real. That was your aim, wasn't it?'

Skye opened her mouth but she suddenly dropped her head into her hands. 'I must have been mad…'

'Agreed,' he replied with unflattering promptness.

'So…' Skye raised her head, her eyes widening '…you weren't serious?'

'Oh, I was.' But the look he cast her was distinctly mocking. 'We're two people who still have a rather odd effect on each other considering the lengths we go to to prove otherwise. But we are playing with fire, Skye.'

She moistened her lips. 'Because…?'

He pulled up outside her home, switched the engine off and laid his head back. 'Because, damn it,' he said almost to himself, 'I may be at loggerheads with my father at the moment but I still admire and respect him and I hate deceiving him. Because I didn't expect you of all people to—to be party to it, and because, Skye—' he raised his head abruptly '—we still can't keep our hands off each other.'

'I feel terrible,' Skye said uncertainly, and swallowed several times. 'But may I explain something? It was…' she paused and cleared her throat as she tried to marshal her thoughts '…it was a women united against men kind of thing.'

He laughed but not pleasantly.

'Your mother is distraught, your sister was the same—there seemed to be no way to get through to either you or your father and I was the one who seemed to have done most of the damage,' she said despairingly.

'And what did you plan to do after Pippa's wedding?' he enquired. 'Another bout of tears at an airport?'

'Nick,' she said on a breath.

'What, as a matter of interest, do you think that would have done to my relationship with my father?'

Skye started to speak a couple of times then she burst out, '*Why?* I can't understand why he's taken it so very badly. There are other women—'

'I told you,' he said grimly. 'The whole bloody country has fallen in love with you—'

'That's not true!' she protested.

'No?' He looked at her cynically. 'Even when you were hiding yourself on Haggerstone Island you came up with one. Look, I don't mean Dad's physically in love with you but you couldn't have fulfilled his vision of the perfect daughter-in-law better. That's how much everyone loves you, Skye. You're wholesome, you embody the kind of womanly skills older men set a lot of score by but you're no fool. Then there's the way you look.'

She fumbled for the door handle blindly. 'Well, it's just a pity you didn't realize what a perfect wife I'd make, Nick. It's just a pity *you* are the one person in the whole country—and that's really ironic—who doesn't need half the things I am or a quarter even; only one thing and that happens to be sex.'

He sat up abruptly and pressed the central locking device on his door so that her button flew down. 'That's what most marriages are about, Skye,' he said grimly. 'Don't kid yourself you can get along without it.'

She turned a proud, pale face to him. 'You still don't understand, do you, Nick? Yes, of course it's important—it's vital—but so is something else. Your mother may have been able to live without it; I can't. I need to be your soul mate as well. Now, you can call it clinging if you like but if you want to inhabit some other world where I'm not permitted I will call it something else—a fear of true commitment.'

They stared at each other and the electricity that surged between them was charged with hostility as well as everything else that lay between them.

Until she went on at last, 'So, if you're about to suggest we get back together again so you don't have to go on deceiving your father, the answer is no, Nick. But if you have any feeling of compassion for the rest of your family you'll do *something* to ease this crisis. Why don't you just come clean and explain to Mr Hunter why you are the way you are?'

The only sound that followed was that of the button on her door popping up. She shrugged, opened the door and slipped out of the car. It roared away before she'd got her key into her front door.

She swam up from a deep sleep because someone was banging on that same front door the next morning. A groggy glance at her watch showed her it was ten o'clock, not so surprising considering how long it had taken her to get to sleep. She also remembered she'd taken her phone off the hook.

It was her mother who ran up stairs when she'd released the front door.

'What is it?' Skye asked anxiously, clutching her cotton robe around her. 'Has the restaurant blown up? Did the new chef burn everything or serve it raw?' They'd started a new chef the night before.

'No, no, he was fine. Skye, I think you should sit down,' Iris said. 'By the way I tried to phone you but you were always engaged.'

'Oh, I took the phone off the hook.'

'Why?' Iris stared at her suspiciously. 'How did it go last night?'

'Um—OK. Mum, what's all this about?'

'No scenes, no rows, no…anything?'

'No! Well, not that I know of. Why?'

Iris swallowed. 'I just heard a news flash. Richard Hunter died in his sleep last night.'

'Are you all right? Drink this, darling—you look so pale.'

It was a stiff shot of brandy Iris handed her daughter. Skye took a sip. 'I can't believe it! He was fine and he was only in, well, his sixties, I presume.'

'Sixty-nine. There was a short resume of his life. It was a heart attack.'

Skye put the back of her hand to her mouth and her eyes were anguished. 'Nick will be…'

'Perhaps you should go to him,' Iris suggested.

'Oh, no. I...no.' Skye closed her eyes in pain. 'I'm the last person he'd want to see at the moment.'

Iris sighed then hugged her daughter.

A week later, after a private funeral to which Skye had sent flowers but otherwise had no contact with the Hunter family, Pippa came to see her again.

'I don't know how to tell you how sorry I am,' Skye said to her as she led her into the lounge. 'You must be...well, I can imagine. Please sit down.'

Pippa sank into an armchair. 'Of course I'm terribly sad,' she said, 'but...none of us could have helped it and—he didn't die unhappy.'

Skye's eyes widened.

'That's why I had to come and thank you, Skye,' Pippa said. 'That night, after everyone left, he took me aside and...and we talked, as we used to. He told me that the most important thing for him was for *me* to be happy, and he gave me his blessing. We were at peace with each other, Skye, and that means so much to me even though he's gone.' She put her hands gently on her belly. 'I know the way you were that night with Jean-Claude must have helped. He admired you so much.'

Skye blinked away some tears and found she couldn't speak.

'The other thing is—and Mum asked me to tell you this—before they fell asleep that night, she was able to talk to him about Nick for the first time since this all blew up. Talk rationally and openly. And he told her that he'd been an old fool because he could see Nick slipping away from him but it had only occurred to him that night that *he* was doing the pushing but there was something he didn't understand riding him. Something that made him want to see his family settled.'

Skye stared at her with her lips parted. 'Did he have some sort of premonition?'

'We don't know but it's possible he had some symptoms he was hiding even from himself. But he and Mum…she said, before they fell asleep, they got closer than they'd ever been. It's something that's sustained her and maybe always will.'

Skye reached for her hanky this time and wept quietly for a moment. Then she raised her tear-streaked face to Pippa. 'And Nick?'

'There's nothing much sustaining Nick at the moment, I'm afraid. Oh, you need to know him well to be able to see it but…' She shrugged. 'We've cancelled the wedding, in the form it was going to be in, at least. It'll be very small and private in a fortnight.'

'Where…is Nick?' Skye asked.

'In Melbourne on business at the moment. I think he gets back in a couple of days.'

Skye was restless, sad and troubled over the next two days.

She couldn't settle to her book, she wandered around her flat touching her plants then indulged in an orgy of repotting. Although she and Pippa hadn't said a lot more they'd parted with warmth and deep affection—and just before she'd turned to go Pippa had added one thing. Nick's flight number, the date and the time he was due back in Sydney.

'I got it from Flo,' she'd said, and stood poised to say more but in the end she'd kissed Skye on the cheek and left.

Not the airport, Skye said to herself over and over. If she was going to do anything it had to be done privately. But how and where? Should she ring him? Should she leave a message on his answering machine?

Then an idea crept into her mind and she went to check her keyring. The security key and the doorkey to Nick's apartment were still there although she'd forgotten she had them. For that matter, she mused, he still had a set of keys to her flat.

She sat down with the keyring clutched tightly in her hand. What if...say he came home with Wynn? What if he was as angry as he'd been the night of the party? Or more so because he'd lost his father while he was still in discord with him?

Could she rely on Pippa's summing up of his state of mind? Because the more she thought about it, the more obvious it became that Pippa had been urging her to do this. But Pippa had no way of knowing how badly they'd fallen out again, or the special significance it had in the context of his father's death.

Then the day he was due home dawned, and suddenly all her uncertainty left her. Not that she was sure that she was doing the right thing, but she couldn't rid herself of the deep desire to go to him whatever the consequences.

So she made her plans. His flight was due in at five o'clock in the afternoon. She let herself into his apartment at four.

CHAPTER EIGHT

SHE made her preparations carefully then stood looking around his lounge.

She'd always liked his apartment despite what she'd said when they'd first parted. After all, she reminded herself, it had been like a second home to her for a time. But it was strange to come back to it, and alone.

She felt as if she was trespassing. Who else had sat in his luxurious beige suede settees and chairs? Or sat cross-legged on the cinnamon carpet? Perhaps piled up the colourful scatter cushions in ochre, burnt sienna, sage-green and lain back against them, or pulled the heavy oyster curtains closed although there was no need except to give a sense of added intimacy.

Who else had known him well enough to rearrange his collection of rocks, crystal and quartz, look for a book in the glass-fronted bookcases or simply run her fingers along the lovely satiny wood of the occasional tables and other pieces, some antiques worth a fortune?

Who had brought flowers, then, because the one thing his apartment had lacked was anything resembling a vase, had bought him six, ranging from pottery urns to chunky square cut glass and one to-die-for Moorcroft vase?

Her thoughts moved on to the kitchen where she'd

stocked his pantry with dried herbs and spices, lima
beans, sesame oil, sweet-chilli sauce and a whole host
of ingredients he would never have thought to buy
for himself, as well as installing an electric wok.

Which left one essential room in the apartment to
wander over in her mind: the master bedroom.

He'd always been slightly ambivalent about his
bedroom, as if the black and gold magnificence cre-
ated by an interior decorator didn't quite sit easily
with him. The carpet was black with a band of buttery
cream running around the bed. The furniture was exquisite—two Hepplewhite mahogany armchairs cov-
ered in straw velvet, a bow-fronted walnut bureau and
bedhead—and there was black and gold linen on the
bed. A magnificent gold-framed mirror hung on one
wall.

Skye had stopped to blink several times the first
time she'd crossed the threshold.

He'd laughed and explained that, while he'd ex-
erted a restraining influence and got the rest of the
apartment done to his taste, this bedroom had got
away from him while he was overseas and he'd never
got around to changing it.

Had Wynn, she wondered now, when she'd first
seen it, laughed with him or…?

She snatched her thoughts away deliberately.

At six o'clock, she heard a key turn in the lock.

She was sitting curled up on a settee paging
through a magazine, and she froze. Her limbs actually
seemed to lock and the magazine slid soundlessly to
the thickly carpeted floor. She could see through to

the entrance hall of Nick's apartment but because of the angle she wouldn't be visible unless he turned.

So she watched as he dropped his bag to the floor, shrugged off his jacket and loosened his tie. Then he went still, and sniffed. The faint, delicious aroma of roast lamb and rosemary was on the air—his favourite dish and the very first one she'd cooked for him.

He turned slowly, his eyes sweeping the lounge, and at last she found the strength to stand up as they came to rest on her.

He blinked, as if he thought he was seeing a mirage, and she bit her lip because he looked so different. Pale, strained—as if his nerves were stretched beyond the limit—thinner, even gaunt.

'What's…this?' he said.

Skye smoothed the skirt of her button-through chalk-blue dress, and did the only thing she was capable of. She held out her hand.

'Oh, no,' he said, and closed his eyes briefly. 'Not again, Skye.'

'What do you mean?' she asked huskily.

'I mean you may be able to make love to me and walk away from me but I'm…' He stopped and gritted his teeth.

Skye moved and came to stand a few paces from him. 'I don't intend to ever walk away from you again, Nick.'

He scanned her from top to toe. The way her hair was tied back simply, the way her dress with its heart-shaped neck skimmed her figure and fell in folds about her calves, her low-heeled blue sandals. But he said dryly, 'Why? What do you think has changed apart from the obvious?'

'I've changed,' she answered quietly. 'I can't bear to think of you suffering without me being there to help. I… Whatever you can give, Nick, is enough for me because the fact of the matter is, I can't live without you.'

'Skye, we don't change basically. You're still the girl who didn't really like to live dangerously and—and you accused me of this once—feeling guilty is no reason to come back to me.'

'But I don't feel guilty.'

'Don't you? I sure as hell do.' He turned away and pulled off his tie.

'What about?' she whispered.

He turned back, running the navy blue strip of silk through his fingers. 'About letting him go to bed thinking you and I were getting back together. About—letting anyone or anything come between us because there's no way, nor is there ever going to be a way, to rectify things.'

Skye licked her lips. 'Have you spoken to your mother?'

'Yes,' he said wearily. 'I presume you have too—'

'No, Pippa.'

'Whoever, but that doesn't mean a great deal to me. Look, I'm happy for my mother and I'm happy for Pip but *I* didn't get the opportunity to straighten things with him myself so it's not the same.'

'Nick, your father deserves better than this.'

His dark eyes grew sardonic. 'What would you

know about it, Skye? What would you know about losing someone through your own stupidity—'

'Because that's how I nearly came to lose you, Nick,' she broke in. 'I wanted perfection but it doesn't exist. And losing your father brought that home to me. Life is too short and precarious to be making mountains out of molehills. So if loving you is also going to be living dangerously, so be it.'

The faintest smile touched his mouth but it was gone almost immediately. 'That's easy to *say*, Skye, not so easy to live. And don't think I don't appreciate this but half of it still has to be motivated by guilt— we set out to deceive him so how can we assuage that guilt? By doing what he would have wanted.'

'I set out to deceive him, Nick, not you. And I did it along with your sister and your mother, both of whom also loved him dearly.'

'I gave a pretty fair imitation of it.'

She paused for a moment, trying to regroup, trying to find the key to break through his defences. 'All right, let's examine that. If you did give a pretty fair imitation of it, might it have been because you couldn't help yourself?'

'Skye, I saw you rubbing your wrist that night and I know I must have left bruises on it. I was also dead angry underneath.'

'I remember,' she said quietly, and involuntarily put the fingers of one hand around her other wrist. 'But perhaps it wasn't only because we were deceiving him. Perhaps it was to do with…*you* wanting it to be real as much as he did.'

He was grimly silent for a long moment.

She took advantage of it to add, 'You did say only just now that you couldn't make love to me and walk away—not that it was ever easy to walk away from you, Nick. In fact it was the hardest thing I've ever done, so don't be deceived into thinking otherwise.'

He shrugged and turned away from her. 'I don't know about you but I need a drink.'

Skye swallowed and clasped her hands, then she went back to the settee and sat down.

Presently he came back and put a glass of wine down beside her. He'd poured himself a rather dark looking Scotch and he sat opposite her in the same low armchair he'd been occupying the first time she'd ever laid eyes on him, and been so determined to be unimpressed by him.

She took a sip of her wine and put the glass down resolutely.

Causing him to eye her with amusement, and say, 'That looked ominous, Skye. I gather you're about to lecture me again?'

She froze then made an effort to pull herself together. 'Not necessarily,' she murmured. 'Certainly not if you intend to act like a brick wall.'

He raised a lazy eyebrow at her. 'Retreat, then? That would be unkind, at least before you've fed me.'

'As a matter of fact none of those things, Nick. No,' she said thoughtfully, although inside she was both angry and determined, and quite aware that a devil was riding her but unable to do a thing about it. 'No, I thought I might—live a little dangerously, Nick.' Her eyes glinted with sheer irony. 'Like this.'

She stood up and took off the band tying her hair

back, and ran her fingers through the free curls. Then she slowly and unconcernedly began to free each little button down the front of her dress.

She heard him take a sharp breath but she didn't even look at him.

It was by the time she'd reached her waist that he said sardonically, 'I get the picture, Skye, but should we stop and try to work out whether this is Skye Belmont, TV personality, or the real girl?'

Her fingers stilled and she looked into his dark eyes calmly. 'Nick, there may be some differences between me and that girl on TV, but taking my clothes off for a man is not something either of us would do unless we really wanted to.' And she bent her head and began to undo the buttons down the skirt of her dress.

He had another shot at her. He laid his head back and drawled, 'On the other hand, you have told me that a lot of the things you did with me were done by that other girl because that's how you thought I wanted you to be.'

Skye came to the last button and slipped it free. She straightened and the dress fell open, revealing her white bra and bikini briefs. She bent again to slip off her sandals. Then she paused and looked at him very directly, and all of a sudden her anger, her devil and every other contrary emotion drained away, leaving her sure of just one thing...

She eased the dress off, laid it over the back of the settee, and walked over to him. The afternoon sun gave her a golden glow so that her hair was fairer than ever and her skin looked luminous and silky. Her legs were long and slim, her waist tiny above the triangle of white silk and lace, her arms and shoulders smooth and delicate.

His dark gaze drifted over her as it had that very first time, only this time she saw him clench his hands and knew it was only an incredible effort of will that kept him in his chair.

She reached behind her and unclasped her bra, freeing her breasts so they lay on her body like ripe, luscious fruit tipped with velvet peaks. Then she sank down onto her knees in front of him, picked up his hand and placed it on her heart.

'Nick,' she said huskily, 'this is the real me, taking the kind of risk I would never have dreamt of because—it's the only way I could think of to get through to you the fact that I love you, I never stopped even when I did walk away for what seem like trivial reasons now, and I never will stop loving you.'

He didn't move and there were harsh lines scored in his face, there was disbelief in his eyes—and there was a tell-tale nerve jumping beside the hard set of his mouth.

'Do you know what Bryce said to me when we parted?' Skye went on in that barely audible, husky voice.

She felt his fingers tighten on her skin beneath her hand and she saw a kind of sceptical incredulity come to his eyes, but she went on steadily, 'He said he'd worked out that I was the kind of girl who only gave herself to one man. He was right.'

'Skye…' he said her name on a tortured breath '…there's still so much that wouldn't work—'

'No, my darling, there's only this,' she murmured, and lifted his hand to her mouth. 'The rest can all be worked out somehow.'

There was only a moment more of indecision, as if he was fighting the hardest battle of his life, then, with a groan, he pulled her into his arms. 'I swore,' he said indistinctly into her hair, 'I didn't need you, Skye, because I didn't think I could ever get you back after…'

'It's in the past now,' Skye whispered.

'Yes, but I didn't even know, really know, what I'd done to myself until you walked out on me on Lizard. Because my pride wouldn't let me admit that all the things I *prided* myself on were…like ashes in my mouth without you.'

She lifted her face to his and all the old love, excitement and adoration were in them.

So much so that he held her against him so she could barely breathe.

'There's more,' he warned, loosening his arms with a sigh. 'I could have killed Bryce Denver when I thought of him…being clumsy with you or hurting you. I could cheerfully have incarcerated Wynn in a convent when I realized what I'd so thoughtlessly got myself into, but did I stop to ask myself why? No,' he marvelled.

'Nick—'

'Hush, sweetheart,' he murmured, and kissed her on the mouth. 'I need to let you know what a blind, bloody idiot I was. What did I do? I tried to push you into Bryce's arms; I actually told you I should never have started anything with you; I soldiered on with

Wynn, although I never did go to bed with her or anyone else after we parted, Skye.'

'I'm so glad,' she said simply.

'But I did all that out of…rage, only I didn't understand what it was at the time. Rage that I could have been such a fool. Rage battling pride and leaving this cold, empty space within that made me do things I'll always regret.'

'Nick—' she sat up in the circle of his arms '—don't think you were alone. I can remember telling you I thought Wynn would be much better for you than I ever could be—out of the same kind of emotion. Because I knew in my heart I didn't believe one word of it, and it was sheer hell just watching you dance with her.'

'I see.' The faintest smile touched his lips and he fiddled with a curl of her hair.

They eyed each other then they were laughing together, kissing lightly then more and more passionately, and finally there was only one thing more to do.

'I love this bed and this room,' she said dreamily, quite a time later.

He held her in his arms and looked around his bedroom ruefully. 'Well, it's comfortable—'

'It's more than that. It's where you first made love to me and it's where we came back to each other. I think we'll always keep this bed and this decor, Nick.'

He nuzzled her neck. 'It so happens I'm in complete agreement. You were sensational.'

'So were you.' Skye sighed rapturously because

their lovemaking had been in fact not dramatic but more tender and exquisitely slow than ever before. A true union of hearts, minds and bodies, a drinking in of all the things they loved about each other, a time to say things they'd never said before. All the same it had left them wordless and clinging to each other, emotionally and physically moved as they never had been before.

'Do you remember what you said to me once about fantastic sex making you starv...? Oh, no!' Skye sat up with a hand to her mouth.

He sat up beside her and took her hand, but he was laughing. 'Don't tell me you've never burnt dinner before?'

'Never—Nick, we could be burning the place down!'

'I doubt it but shall we go and see?'

'I'll go and get my dress—'

But he pulled her back into his arms. 'You don't need to.'

'I...well, I do know I've taken to living dangerously but—' She paused.

'Being naked in the kitchen is a different matter?' he suggested gravely. 'Don't forget you did it beautifully in the lounge.'

'I've got the feeling you're never going to let me forget—what I did,' she replied equally gravely.

'You could be right.'

'Nick—' she turned a laughing face to his '—just don't remind me in public. I have the greatest difficulty not to go all weak at the knees when you only look at me in a certain way as it is.'

'I think that's just about the nicest thing you've ever said to me.' He was still being grave but what lurked in his eyes was another matter.

She swallowed and touched her fingers to his mouth. 'We should at least check the kitchen first.'

'All right.' He looked comically rueful. 'But the reason you don't need your dress is because of this.' He released her and got up to go to the built-in wardrobe. From it he drew a yellow silk robe. Hers.

Skye's eyes widened. 'I left it, didn't I? I didn't mean to. When I got home I remembered throwing it over a chair and…and…I thought you'd probably thrown it away.'

'No.' He sat down beside her. 'I couldn't bring myself to. It still had—still has the perfume of your skin on it. In really desperately dark moments I haven't been able to stop myself from taking it out and—wishing to high heaven that I had you in my arms.'

'Oh, Nick.' She brushed sudden tears from her eyes. 'I think that's the nicest thing you've said to me.'

They inspected the roast lamb together.

It was a shrunken, blackened piece of inedible meat.

They looked at each other and burst out laughing.

'It may have to be an omelette; think you can survive on that?' Skye asked. 'There's not a whole lot else to work with.'

'Whatever you cook is always magical, Skye, but

you don't have to rush. Should we continue living dangerously for a while?'

'Do you mean go back to bed?'

'Since that provides food for my soul, my darling, in a word, yes.'

She went straight into his arms.

Much later, when they'd showered together and Skye had cooked an omelette and they were eating it overlooking the view of the harbour, he said, 'You were right.'

She raised an eyebrow at him.

'About my father's memory deserving more.' He picked up his wine glass and sat back with it. 'I feel at peace with him at last.'

'I'm so glad but—only over us?'

He shook his head. 'I may do things differently, I may do them my way; that's been part of the problem—trying to weld our two visions together. He tended to look back, I tended to look forward. Natural, I guess, but I think that's why I was so— restless. But I'll never forget all the things he taught me or his basic wisdom, and the fact that he cared enough to know what was best for me even when I didn't.'

Skye said nothing but she raised her glass and touched it to his.

'I see.'

Twelve months on, Richard Kenneth Hunter, named for his two grandfathers, had not long previously made his way into the world, causing his father to make that comment.

Skye, sitting up in bed with her new son in her arms, looked at her husband a shade warily. 'What does that mean?'

Nick closed the door of her private room, which was already resembling a hothouse, took his shoes off and got onto the bed to sit beside Skye. He stretched his long legs out, put an arm round her shoulders, and murmured, 'You don't still doubt me in any way, do you, Mrs Hunter?'

Skye leant back against him. Her pregnancy had been trouble-free, her labour not too arduous and Nick had been wonderful all the way through. Just being married to him had been wonderful. The places she'd feared she'd never be able to reach in him hadn't, after all, existed.

There'd been times when he'd had to be away from her, and she'd made another TV series—her last for the time being—but it was always as if an invisible cord had bound them together.

This, though, was the one thing she hadn't been able to quite clear of a feeling of wariness—that this was the reality that might just change things...

'I...no,' she said slowly. 'You've been so wonderful, Nick.' She stopped uncertainly.

'But you still can't quite forget what I said about children?'

She shrugged and laid her cheek on her son's. He was fast asleep and, even at only a few hours old, was giving every indication that he would take after his father.

'Then—may I hold him for a while?'

Skye's eyes widened. 'I'm not that good at it myself yet.'

'He doesn't seem to be showing any disapproval.'

Skye hesitated then passed the bundle carefully over to Nick—who held the baby as if he were breakable for a moment then made himself comfortable with Master Richard Kenneth lodged securely in the crook of his arm. He even, with his other hand, rearranged the blue bunny rug around his son so that more of him was visible. Richard pursed his lips but didn't open his eyes and slept on serenely.

'Nick!' Skye stared at him with the light of laughter dawning in her eyes. 'You look as if you're an old hand at this.'

'Not by any means,' he responded. 'But this is my son and heir. This baby doesn't know it but as soon as he's old enough we're going to do some camping out under the stars, we're going to look for lumps of rock, I'm going to tell him the stories his grandfather used to tell me. One thing I'm not going to do, though, is weigh him down with the pressures of an empire unless he wants it.'

Skye could only stare at him, tears in her eyes.

He reached for her hand. 'The other thing he will always be aware of, as will any brothers and sisters he may have, is the unlimited admiration and love I have for his mother.'

'And I for you,' she said, and sighed with absolute relief and love as he drew her back against him.

The world's bestselling romance series.

HARLEQUIN®
Presents~

Seduction and Passion Guaranteed!

We are pleased to announce
Sandra Marton's fantastic new series

The
O'CONNELLS

In order to marry, they've got to gamble on love!

Don't miss...

KEIR O'CONNELL'S MISTRESS

Keir O'Connell knew it was time to leave Las Vegas when he became consumed with desire for a dancer. The heat of the desert must have addled his brain! He headed east and set himself up in business— but thoughts of the dancing girl wouldn't leave his head. And then one day there she was, Cassie...

Harlequin Presents #2309
On sale March 2003

Pick up a Harlequin Presents® novel and you will enter a world of spine-tingling passion and provocative, tantalizing romance!

Available wherever Harlequin books are sold.

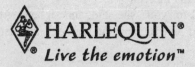

HARLEQUIN®
Live the emotion™

Visit us at www.eHarlequin.com

HPTOCON

The world's bestselling romance series.

HARLEQUIN®
Presents

Seduction and Passion Guaranteed!

Your dream ticket to the vacation of a lifetime!

Why not relax and allow Harlequin Presents® to whisk you away
to stunning international locations with our new miniseries...

Where irresistible men and sophisticated women surrender to seduction under the golden sun.

Don't miss this opportunity to experience glamorous lifestyles and exotic settings in:

This Month:
MISTRESS OF CONVENIENCE
by Penny Jordan
on sale August 2004, #2409

Coming Next Month:
IN THE ITALIAN'S BED
by Anne Mather
on sale September 2004, #2416

Don't Miss!
THE MISTRESS WIFE
by Lynne Graham
on sale November 2004, #2428

FOREIGN AFFAIRS... A world full of passion!

**Pick up a Harlequin Presents® novel and you will enter a world
of spine-tingling passion and provocative, tantalizing romance!**

Available wherever Harlequin books are sold.

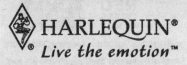

HARLEQUIN®
Live the emotion™

www.eHarlequin.com   HPFAUPD

On sale now

girls' night in

21 of today's hottest
female authors
1 fabulous short-story collection
And all for a good cause.

Featuring *New York Times* bestselling authors

Jennifer Weiner (author of *Good in Bed*),
Sophie Kinsella (author of *Confessions of a Shopaholic*),
Meg Cabot (author of *The Princess Diaries*)

Net proceeds to benefit War Child, a network of organizations
dedicated to helping children affected by war.

Also featuring bestselling authors...

Carole Matthews, Sarah Mlynowski, Isabel Wolff, Lynda Curnyn,
Chris Manby, Alisa Valdes-Rodriguez, Jill A. Davis, Megan McCafferty,
Emily Barr, Jessica Adams, Lisa Jewell, Lauren Henderson,
Stella Duffy, Jenny Colgan, Anna Maxted, Adele Lang,
Marian Keyes and Louise Bagshawe

www.RedDressInk.com   www.WarChildusa.org

Available wherever trade paperbacks are sold.

RDIGNIMM

eHARLEQUIN.com
The Ultimate Destination for Women's Fiction

Visit eHarlequin.com's Bookstore today for today's most popular books at great prices.

- An extensive selection of romance books by top authors!

- Choose our convenient "bill me" option. No credit card required.

- New releases, Themed Collections and hard-to-find backlist.

- A sneak peek at upcoming books.

- Check out book excerpts, book summaries and Reader Recommendations from other members and post your own too.

- Find out what everybody's reading in Bestsellers.

- Save BIG with everyday discounts and exclusive online offers!

- Our Category Legend will help you select reading that's exactly right for you!

- Visit our Bargain Outlet often for huge savings and special offers!

- Sweepstakes offers. Enter for your chance to win special prizes, autographed books and more.

Your purchases are 100% guaranteed—so shop online at www.eHarlequin.com today!

INTBB104

The world's bestselling romance series.

HARLEQUIN®
Presents~

Seduction and Passion Guaranteed!

Legally wed,
Great together in bed,
But he's never said…
"I love you"

They're…

Wedlocked!

**The series
where marriages
are made in
haste…and love
comes later….**

Don't miss
HIS CONVENIENT MARRIAGE by Sara Craven #2417
on sale September 2004

Coming soon
MISTRESS TO HER HUSBAND by Penny Jordan #2421
on sale October 2004

**Pick up a Harlequin Presents® novel and you will
enter a world of spine-tingling passion and
provocative, tantalizing romance!**

Available wherever Harlequin books are sold.

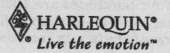

HARLEQUIN®
Live the emotion™

www.eHarlequin.com   HPWEDSO